The Legacies of
Darkness

WILLIAM DE PAOLA

THE LEGACIES OF DARKNESS

Four

Thrilling Short Stories in One Book!

Unique stories that offer readers a special twist that they are going to love!

authorHOUSE®

AuthorHouse™ LLC
1663 Liberty Drive
Bloomington, IN 47403
www.authorhouse.com
Phone: 1-800-839-8640

Published by AuthorHouse 01/06/2014

ISBN: 978-1-4685-4780-1 (sc)
ISBN: 978-1-4685-4779-5 (e)

Library of Congress Control Number: 2012901411

Contents

THE ENDING

Synopsis: Being a boss of a group of thugs and gangsters is a ritual of years of formed habits that throughout the years form a mold to either be a pawn or a wolf. There are reasons you go down a path—that reason is your destiny. Do you make it through the levels it takes to be a boss? Are you going to be taken advantage of? Or are you a leader who is respected and not betrayed?

The End

Chapter I

The Beginning

Maybe it was meant to be, but one would not normally believe that the world one lived in and rules could come toppling down in a matter of minutes! When that time came, how would he feel? Would he be brave, or would he be scared? Who would be there with him? Should he end it where and how he wanted, or how they wanted? Or would it be a matter of character and circumstance?

These were Angelo's thoughts and he knew as a mob boss he could count on only a few to be with him!

The countdown was on; everything was falling apart before his very eyes. There had been signs, but he failed to recognize them, and now he was looking on in disbelief, thinking about which direction to go.

They were in front of the house! Angelo looked down at them from a large window in the old colonial-style home located on a large corner lot in a quiet part of Chicago. It was a large home, having eight bedrooms, but it was ideally sized for a large family and for his base of operations. The house had been modified to his personal specifications, accommodating any possible scenario he could think of regarding treachery within his family, or any attack from without by rivals in his business.

The sun was just starting to rise; the usually calm street was now filled with police activity, and one could hear the sound of helicopters flying overhead. The Boss could not believe what he was looking at.

The emotion of being the hunted started to settle in. The sweat on his forehead ran down the side of his face, and he wiped it away with a handkerchief. The only other people in the room were his beautiful wife of over ten years and his trusted consigliere, Joe. As his wife and Joe looked at each other, they waited for Angelo to say something to reassure them, for his guidance, but he just stared quietly out the window.

Looking back to how this could have happened, what was the downfall that would now bring his empire to an end? Angelo wore a smirk as he remembered that special someone he would miss the most; Gloria a spectacularly beautiful woman he was introduced to six years before at a private gathering, and very quickly, Glo as he liked to call her became for Angelo like a drug he couldn't do without. There was an exotic wild side to Gloria; she had a charm unlike any woman he had ever known and the class to fit in anywhere.

As the years passed and he spent more time with Gloria, Angelo gained a lot of power in his world. There were many business deals, his organization was growing in money and man power. Everything was looking up for Angelo. There was always time for Natalie his beautiful and trusting wife, but on special nights the boss looked forward to being with Gloria.

Something always lingered inside him to be with her; she made him feel confident that he could do anything. It was like she was his special angel, and it worked well for Angelo for his confidence and his character; it helped him as he rose higher in the mafia's tough world.

All these things Angelo thought about while Natalie, and his consigliere, Joe waited for some response from him. He stopped reminiscing and looked over at the two of them and gave one last order, first to Joe, his consigliere. "Go! They came for me. There is nothing they can do to you, remember all we talked about if this day should come. Make sure my family is taken care of and that you follow all I told you to do. The lawyers are down there waiting, and they will take good care of you." Joe hugged Angelo tightly and said, "good luck boss" Joe gave Angelo a look of deep respect and then he left the room.

Natalie stood and stared at Angelo, with tears in her eyes, the husband she had loved and trusted so much, waiting for guidance as she has done since the first time they had met.

Natalie had met her husband more than ten years before at a private dinner party held in Angelo's honor. She was standing at the bar with her uninspiring date. When Angelo made his entrance into the dining room, everyone's attention including Natalie's went directly to him. He was a man who carried himself with an aura of both power and danger. She watched him make his rounds and after a few minutes of making his introduction, while shaking hands with one of the guests he noticed her, and he couldn't turn away. They made long eye contact, and at that moment and without hesitation Angelo came over and introduced himself. Not caring who she was with, it was at that moment she made a decision that changed her life forever; he asked her to please come sit with him and have a drink as he held his hand out for her, looking into Angelo's eyes she gladly accepted. From that first day Natalie knew he would be the only man she would ever love.

CHAPTER II

THE GETAWAY!

Angelo stood silently looking at his distressed wife. He had two choices and he had to decide quickly: whether to make a getaway or go down, face the police, and try to beat this bullshit rap they were trying to pin on him this time. The racing of his heart and mind made more sweat roll down the side of his face; he again pressed the handkerchief to his face and to his forehead.

He tried to look confident as he looked at his wife, "looking deeply into her eyes as he did the first time they met, I'm sorry for all this. I love you very much, but I need you to trust me. I need you to go down with Joe; they cannot do anything to you they only want me." Angelo gave his wife a long hug and a kiss good-bye, "I love you very much, and don't worry I will see you again!"

Natalie respected her husband's words, and as she turned slowly away and started to leave the room, she looked back at him, worried this might be the last time she would ever see him.

Angelo called to her one more time, though seemingly it was also to reassure himself. "Don't worry, everything will be okay!" And then she was gone.

He looked back out to the street for a quick moment and then quickly closed the thick curtains that covered the windows. He quickly walked over to the large bookcase and pulled out a special book that slowly opened the bookcase up, revealing a small, dark room. He entered the dark room and turned the light switch on. On a small table was an old looking snub-nose pistol, a sawed off shotgun, and a small, black leather suitcase that was open and filled with a large amount of money.

Walking over to the table, he was startled momentarily when the bookcase finished shutting and made a loud click. He quietly said to himself, "Everything will be okay!" reassuring himself he made the right decision. Putting the pistol in the backside of his belt, one hand took the briefcase and the other hand took the shotgun. He was ready to go!

He left the secret room and walked down into a dark tunnel, as he had done many times before, but this time it seemed to take longer. The tunnel finally ended, and there was a ladder leading up.

Angelo thought for a moment of his wife and his consigliore, Joe and what they must be going through at this very minute. He reassured himself again that they would be okay. "They have nothing on them, they are only going to try and harass them, those fucking pigs!" He began to get angry at the position they were in and he was now in. He began to climb up the ladder.

When he reached the top, he stood quietly in a dark room and listened for a minute. He heard nothing but a TV. Then he slowly opened the backside of a bookcase revealing a view of a large, upscale bedroom.

There was a king-size bed with black silk sheets on it, and women's clothing hung in plain sight. He looked around and saw no sign of anyone but Gloria, only his beautiful mistress lying there, still in bed and under the sheets, unaware that she now had company.

Angelo cleared his throat, and Gloria looked quickly over at him. She was startled to see him standing there, especially with the shotgun in his hand. He held his finger up to his mouth for her to be quiet.

He could only imagine what was going through her innocent mind. Angelo said quietly, "Get dressed and let's go! It's not going to be safe staying here anymore."

Gloria got up, wearing only a pair of red silk pajama pants. She knew he was serious and rushed around to get dressed. As she got ready, she hurried around the room grabbing whatever clothes were lying around, throwing them into a suitcase. Angelo said quietly, "Don't' forget the necklace." He remembered back to when they were on a vacation together as she was packing up her suitcase.

Their 1st vacation together

They were in a luxury hotel in Miami Beach, and he was laying on the bed wearing a robe, watching Gloria, who was dressed in sexy lingerie, packing up her clothes and putting them into a suitcase.

As she was putting the clothing in the suitcase, and under one of the shirts was a medium-size box. She picked it up and looked over at him. Angelo said, "Bring the box and come over here and sit with me." Gloria walked quickly over and sat next to him with a smile on her face, anticipating what was inside. "Open it up!" She got a bigger smile and then turned all her attention back to the box as she carefully opened it.

There was a beautiful diamond necklace and earrings. She looked at it for a moment, amazed. "Thank you, baby it's so beautiful, I love it so much. You're the best!" She gave him a long hug, and they started to kiss. Stopping her for a moment and looking her in the eyes, "The moment I saw you at that party, I knew I had to have you! This is our first real getaway together, and there will be many more to come. I am very happy that you are now part of my life."

The room—Present

She was packed and ready and stood there with a look of uncertainty, holding the suitcase in one hand and a coat in the other. Angelo said, "Let's go!" As they went for the back door, there was a loud noise, someone had just kicked in the front door of the house, and they were now in the next room.

He stopped and pressed her hard up against the wall, almost taking her breath away looking around the corner at who it was. The shotgun was ready to be used at any moment.

It was two police officers; they were now in a dark room with the only light coming through the sides of the curtains. To the unsuspecting officers there was now a sawed-off shotgun pointing at them, and he fired away, blowing a large hole into each one of the officers.

The two policemen now lay bloody on the ground. Pulling out his pistol and said, "I have something more for you, pigs!" He walked over to the first officer, who was screaming out in pain. Standing over him, he aimed the gun at his head, and fired one shot. He hurried to the other officer, who already looked dead, but to make sure, he shot him in the head too.

Grabbing his girlfriend hard by the arm, she was in a state of shock at what she had just witnessed, they headed out the back door for the garage. When they were almost to the garage, she said, "There is a different car there."

Before she could explain, he opened the garage door, and in there was a beautiful new black Mercedes. He said "Get in the fucking car!" Gloria began digging frantically in her purse for the keys and handed them to him, Angelo started the car and seeing the garage door opener on the visor, pushed it and opened the garage door.

Angelo backed out of the garage quickly and headed down the alley, looking around for any police or helicopters, nothing. At the end of the alley, he turned onto a side street.

Sitting there quietly with tear in her eyes, Gloria finally looked over at Angelo and asked, "What's going on? What are we going to do?" Angelo growled, "We have to get to a safe house, that's what's going on!" Panic had started to go through his mind. He reached in his pocket for his handkerchief, frantically wiping his sweating forehead.

He went down one street and then another. Farther down the road he could see some type of police road block. "We have to get off the road, it's not safe!" Driving another minute, he became angrier. "There is nowhere to fucking go!" He panicked and looked back up at the sky for helicopters.

Gloria was in a state of shock and disbelief. Looking over at Gloria, Angelo said in a much calmer voice, *"I'm sorry, honey, for all this. You were never to have seen any of it!"*

She sat there in silence with her head down. Angelo looked everywhere to find somewhere safe to turn, but there was nothing, he lost all sense of calmness and started angrily yelling, "Fucking pigs! I'll kill them all!"

Gloria trying to calm him, reached over and grabbing Angelo by the hand, said, "Baby, I know where to go. You will be safe there." She pointed in the direction he should go.

Angelo, looking at her and saying in a more confident voice, "Okay, baby, I'll trust you. We'll go there. I have no other choice". It was not far; he turned down one street and then down an alley. There were some garages, and she pointed to one. "It's the second on the right," she said.

He stopped the car, and she got out and quickly opened the garage door.

Chapter III

The House

The garage was the size for two cars but was empty, and there was a two-story house in back with outside stairs going up to the second floor. It was a fairly older yellow house. Grabbing the shotgun and putting it inside his coat, he took the brief case. He told her, "Let's go! Lead the way!"

They hurried up the stairs, she opened the door, and they went in. With the shotgun ready, he went through all the rooms like a madman, yelling back at her, "Who lives here? Is there another staircase or something that leads to the house below?"

It was not a very big place: a small kitchen area where they came in, a large living room, and a beautifully decorated bedroom with lots of nice clothes and dresses hanging in the closet. Angelo came over to her and said again, "Baby, who the fuck lives here? And is there another way out of here?"

Gloria was silent, looking down as if afraid to say something. He grabbed her by the arm. "Honey, listen to me, it's okay! It will all be okay! We now have this place where we can hide out for a while. When it settles down out there, we will leave and will make it to a safe house, and everything will be okay. You have to trust me! But please, when I ask you something, you have to answer me."

"No, there is nothing that leads to the downstairs house. The only way is out the front door." Gloria answered in a more frightened tone, "I stay here sometimes!" Standing there looking down at her, she was only 5'3" and 110 pounds; he was a large man at 6'1" and 250 pounds.

Angelo said to her, "Did I hear you right?" She continued to look down as she spoke quietly, "I stay here!"

He grabbed her by the arm, squeezing tighter. "What do you mean? Your place is at the other house, which I pay for. Why would you have this place?" Angelo started to look around as if he might know the reason why.

There was a large picture in a silver frame on top of the TV. Quickly walking over he stared at the picture for a minute. "Who is this fucking guy? What are you doing with him?" He threw the picture against the wall, breaking it into pieces. He had begun to put two and two together: she was playing both of them. Angelo also understood at that moment where that new black Mercedes had come from.

He sat down on the couch, in shock as if he had just received a knockout punch. He angrily put the pistol on the table with the briefcase, telling her, "Get me something cold to drink!" He kept the shotgun pointed at the door.

Looking around the room Angelo kept thinking to himself, "What the fuck! How could I have been so naïve?" Angelo loved this woman like he did his wife but in a different way; being able to do things with her that he couldn't do with his wife. He thought to himself now, how could I have ever thought she was some special angel who had come into my life, how could I not have seen what she really was. Gloria brought the drink back, set it on the table, and said, "Relax and don't worry! There is no one coming here tonight."

Angelo stared at her, speechless, looking like he wanted to strangle her. Later in the night he was still sitting quietly on the couch, ready to fire his weapons if need be. Then he heard noises from outside. He quickly got up and looked out the side window: there were police going up and down the street, checking backyards and garages. Gloria sat in a chair watching Angelo nervously pace back and forth and said, "Don't worry, the car is in my friend's name; they can't trace it!" "That's fucking great! Angelo screamed at her; you know when we get out of here, that boyfriend of yours is fucking dead!"

He grabbed his guns and briefcase and went to the back bedroom, lying down on the bed to try and relax and get some sleep. Gloria came and lay down next to Angelo as she had done many times before, giving him a hug and kiss on the cheek and telling him, "*I'm very sorry for all this, you were never supposed to see any of this!*"

Thinking about how they had so many good times together, how he'd bought her everything she ever needed and wanted, taking her on lavish trips to the best places in the world and treating her like a fucking princess. And now this! He got angrier the more he thought about it. "What a deceitful bitch! She has no respect, to do this to me—I am a boss and this does not happen to a boss. And if the other guy even knew, knew it or not, he is fucking dead! All those years she made me happy! How did I not know? I can at least give her credit: she knew I would find out about her little secret when she took me to this shit box of a place, and she knew I would be angry when I found out but she did it anyway, to keep me safe."

Finally Angelo said to her, "You know, I have everything money, power, respect! A beautiful wife, a beautiful girlfriend, both whom I loved so much! One day I knew it would all end, and I respected that day. Everything has to come to an end. But I never thought it would end like this having my heart ripped out, betrayed by someone I loved and trusted! I was so busy watching my enemies, and all the time I should have been watching you".

"All those years together and the love and fun we shared, and now I have to find out about this!" Angelo lay there unable to sleep; staring up at the ceiling. It was about midnight when he heard someone coming up the stairs. Then there was a hard knock on the door, Angelo quickly pushed Gloria out of bed and said, "Go get the door. If it's who I think it is, there will be a lot of bloodshed tonight."

They got up and he shoved Gloria toward the door, the shotgun ready and pointed at the door. A surreal feeling overcame Angelo as his heart raced! "Is it the cops, or is this going to be her fucking lover? I'll chop his fucking balls off and feed them to her."

He looked around; there was no place to hide in this small apartment no place to make a silent getaway. Loud talking erupted outside, and he could see flashing lights all around like someone was trying to look in. **It was the cops!** "Those fucking pigs!"

No more beautiful home, no more luxury cars, no more lavish trips, no more living the legacy as a big crime boss! There had been many gun battles, power struggles, and deadly business deals throughout the years that he had overcome, and it all made him a very feared and powerful boss. *A true capo dei capi!*

Now it would all end here, with a person who had been so deceitful and in a house he was never supposed to see. More flashlights peered through the windows, and he heard them yell, "We know you're in there!" Gloria screamed through the door; "Get out! There is no one here for you!" Angelo had to give it to her, at least she tried to keep them fucking pigs away.

Angelo clasped the shotgun to him harder, his clammy hands gripping the cold hardened steel, ready to fire it at any moment. He yelled out "They're not taking me alive! I'm not afraid to die; I will die with true dignity! **Thinking** my only regret was seeing and being in this fucking house!"

The police yell louder now. "Open the door or we're breaking it down." Gloria would not open the door, keeping it closed pushing all her weight against it, looking back, as if to get one last look at him.

The police suddenly overpowered her as they shoved the door open, causing her to fall back hard onto the floor. The cops run in quickly with their guns ready to fire, they had found him! They were looking at the barrel of a shotgun, the same shotgun that had killed their brothers in arms. He stood alone in the middle of the room, ready to fire at any moment!

Flashlights now came from everywhere and blinded his vision. Multiple police yelled loudly, "Put down the gun!" Everything was happening so fast, but it was playing out in slow motion. Every move he made was being watched closely. He realized that death was only seconds away, just a slight pull of this trigger, and it would all be over. He shut his eyes and took a deep breath, realizing it was his time to die. *Thinking but I'm not going to be dying alone!*

Angelo waiting patiently, ready to pull that trigger and waiting for that second that would bring his soul to the depths of hell. He inched his finger back; "It's time, I'm ready!" Though blinded by the lights, he heard, "Don't do it!" but he was ready, ready to end this legacy. He looked down: lying on the floor, crying and helpless to move or get up, was the woman who had deceived him. The police were standing all around her.

This once beautiful prize of a woman, his secret lover and once trusted companion, who had lived the best of life, now succumbing to a twisted fate of her own. No matter how good a life one lived, it can change at any given moment!

So it was time, Angelo thought and these pigs will die here also. Angelo's finger pulls slowly back on the trigger and blackness instantly comes as the deafening roar of many pistols going off at once and the sound of one shotgun fills the room!

Laying helpless and paralyzed, taking his last breaths and looking out into the darkness, a black cloud slowly appears with devilish red eyes staring silently down at him, Angelo feels a horrifying sensation over taking his body as a fiery underworld comes to life, awaiting Angelo's final breath, a black hole suddenly appears underneath his lifeless body instantly sucking down his screaming soul.

The end!

The Diablo in the Darkness

Synopsis: This is the story of judgment day for four men: a deadly gang leader, a molesting priest, a rapist killer, and a deadly suicide bomber. Their lives change when they take innocence and make it into their own devious acts of vengeance. When each dies, their souls experience the crossroads of their horrific ways, and they enter into the middle world and it's hellish, fiery under layer, where they experience the greatest horrors and pain imaginable.

Log Line: *There has always been something out there, watching your evil ways, and now your soul has attracted something unimaginably evil!*

The End

CHAPTER I

LET THE INNOCENT LIVE AS ONE; LET THE EVIL LIVE WITH NONE!

The Beginning!

There is a place that souls find themselves once they leave the afterlife. Some souls may go up and some may go down, but there is a middle area to which few get to venture. An evil soul, once entered, has a chance to be saved and re-enter the living world to do good, but not before it is relentlessly cleansed.

There is an endless amount of darkness. Thick smoke fills the air as large, charred black metal containers appear to be coming in and out of thick layers of blackened haze. Large flames start to appear out in the distance, and the haze starts to clear, revealing a view of a dark, diminished city.

In the center of the city is one of the areas highlighted by the flames, exposing a medium-size church that looks like it is partially in shambles. Another area stands out: a huge, grayish colored palace that's sitting on top of a hill toward the outer edge of the city. A large football field is in the center part of the city—no huge lights, no oversized banners, just a large, grayish black stadium that has many torches lit, bringing an evil glow to the field. The last highlighted part of the city is a hellish looking prison that is located on the far side of the city. The prison has two stories with thick metal bars on the windows, and large razor fences surrounding the whole building.

Surrounding the city there seems to be an endless amount of black charred boxes; they are held together by specially formed metal and thick amounts of chains, and some have large evil-looking molds of creatures on them; they are hovering at least 50 feet in the air, They are horrific looking containers of some sort, and it is impossible to know what they are designed to hold. Definitely nothing human can live inside of them! They are stacked two high as far as the eyes can see, disappearing in and out of the thick clouds of haze.

In the distance, a deep reddish glow brightens a few of the containers. Why only a few and not all of them at once? A closer look to one of the black boxes reveals a small hole on the top with thick black bars covering it. The boxes look to be six feet long and three feet high.

There is a noise; it seems to be getting louder. Frightful, terrifying screams come from one of these black boxes! Looking down at the small hole, something seems to be moving. It looks like a blackened finger trying to make its way out of the hole! A piece of ash breaks off, and then another as a blackened finger appears. Through the hole there appears to be the black, ash covered face of someone trying to look out. The helpless screams rings out of its darkness as flames start to embellish the now reddened metal.

In the Box

There is an effort to get out of the excruciating heat, but there's no way out. Every second the box is becoming a darker red; the heat is over whelming, and the thick smoke has a smothering effect. No one hears the desperate screams for help, and there is no one to stop this horrifying torture!

As the box heats, the skin is starting to stick to the burning metal. Flames are protruding through the ash-covered hole. The skin on the face and body is a feeling of sheer pain of being stuck with a million needles at once! The clothing is starting to catch on fire. There is no space to move, no way to get out! Everything touched burns in unimaginable pain!

Short breaths are taken to stop the burning inside the chest. The skin is starting to burn so bad that it's causing the blood to boil out of it. Death is here now, squeezing tighter and tighter and sucking the last drops of life out of you.

It suddenly ends, and all goes black! Awakening! As you begin to shake off the remembrance of the horror of being in that hellish box, your heart is racing out of control. You slowly try to get your senses as you remember that horrifying dream of being burning alive. Standing alone in a dark room, head facing the floor as you drop down to a squatting position, trying to get your composure back. A strange feeling starts to come to you as you look at the floor and then around the room, but you are not able to put a finger on it yet. Slowly it comes to you as you start to become very afraid. A chill comes to you as you begin to remember this place! You have done horrific things in a place like this, once pleasuring your sickened, embellished needs.

A shadow catches your eye, appearing and then disappearing into the next room. There is a smell now in the air—it's of rotting death. The walls are becoming a darkened charred color, and the air grows thick with smoke and floating pieces of burning ash.

There is a nasty taste in your mouth as you breathe in the thick smoke. There is something very evil in here, and you get the feeling that something is watching you! Here in this middle world, there is a chance for your soul! Someone has been remorseful, giving you a second chance to clear all your evil ways and to become new and cleansed soul that will hopefully take a path of good!

It's not a welcoming world or a welcoming time for a rehabilitating soul, but for a chance to leave this debilitating place, the soul will have to begin a special transformation. That evil soul that easily brought death, evil, and pain to the lives of so many innocent victims—those sins can't just be washed away! Suffering will have to be done to the soul, and a relentless amount of it!

Six horrific deaths will have to take place in this middle under world, and when the soul has a chance to leave, it will not know it! Later the right choice will have to be made in the human world. If it's not made, then that evil soul will be forced down to a level that is a hundred times worse than this little rehabilitating vacation, and it will never again receive a chance at redemption.

Every soul that enters this middle world is a "counted soul." That counted soul is one who has brought horrific pain and death to so many others, one who lived life in true evil! The blackened ashed boxes that hover the city are holding each soul till the start of the next act of the visual reformed rehabilitation. The souls are to be cleansed with three burning deaths from the ashed black box, and three horrific deaths of the visual horrors from some of the same acts that had brought horrific pain and death to the lives of so many others.

Once the soul is completely cleansed, the souls are then to be brought back to the upper world, where it will have a second chance to make the right choice! The path of good will allow the soul to stay and live in the upper world. If the time comes and the evilness of the soul comes back and continues the path of evil, then an eternity of darkness will be there waiting for it!

CHAPTER II

THE SOULS FIND DARKNESS

Gang Leader

(Makes is a nick name for making things happen—especially death to rival gang members)

Makes is a leader of a deadly notorious black prison gang. Makes is a nickname for making things happen, especially the deaths of rival gang members. He is talking with four other rival gang leaders outside in "The Lot," as they call it. There has been a lot of deadly fighting going on with the gangs for territory in the prison, but there is a request by the gang leaders to make a truce with each other and have peace around the prison, because there is a brutal war brewing between the gangs, and many are going to die!

Makes is now faced with a tough choice to make! He has the largest and deadliest gang; why should he make a truce? These motherfuckers should join him or die! Back in the cell, he discusses this with his top soldiers. The soldiers are waiting, ready for Makes' decision, waiting for the words of war to bring death to their enemies!

It is time, and Makes speaks up to choose the path that is to be taken. The room is silent. Makes stands over his men, dressed in his tight shirt showing his muscles as they are bulging out; veins are showing in his forehead and neck. Makes is pumped up, ready to give the decision to his readied men. "Soldiers, the decision is going to be war! Death shall come to all our enemies, and I want their leaders' heads at my feet! It all will begin, now!"

Makes says loudly to his second in command, "It's on. Kill everyone that stands in our way." The second says in a stern, confident voice, "Gladly!" and walks out with a sickened smile on his face. "It is time for our massacre to begin!" Makes yells out hysterically to the group.

Pandemonium rings out in the war zone of a prison. Smoke from burning beds cover the air; screams from dying inmates fill the air as gang members stab and brutally beat rivals. A deadly savage war is going on in the prison. Makes sits confidently in his cell and listens. No one is safe, and no one can stop it!

Not long after the deadly decision was made, Makes sits in his cell and waits on his men as they bring him updates. Makes barks orders out as decisions are made to his men. Blood is on the cell walls and all over the prison floors; screams of death ring out all over, and the fierce, brutal attacks go on for an hour.

The fighting is getting closer to Makes' cell. Makes thinks it's almost over and comments to himself, "Good, this will all end shortly, and I will be the true leader in this fucking hell hole of a prison, only me!" Makes didn't realize that it's the rival gangs that are heard getting close, who are the ones that are winning; they have teamed up with each other to take down Makes and his deadly gang.

The fighting is now only a few cells down. Makes smile changes as he listens to what is going on only a few doors down from his cell. He now sits ready with large shanks in each hand, ready to kill if need be.

Two very large soldiers that were standing in front of Makes' cell are now fighting with everything they have. They are trying to hold off the opposing gang no matter the cost, to keep them from touching their leader. The fighting is brutal and horrific, the two large soldiers are stabbed in the face, chest, and hands. They fight for their lives as well as trying to hold the line with everything they got. Overwhelmed, one falls then the other, and they are taken down and brutally stomped and stabbed to death.

Makes is alone in his cell with nowhere to run, looking now at five bloody, deadly enemies standing in front of his cell. These men look ravaged, and their breathing is heavy and labored as they look at their new prey, thirsty for one more kill. There is no stopping these deadly killers; they live every day of their lives for this, because this is their true prize, a rival gang leader and this is their way of life—kill or be killed!

They enter the cell slowly, bloodthirsty knives at the ready. They stare at Makes no one says anything. They approach the once untouchable deadly leader, the one that made the final decision for all this brutality and death to happen. There is nowhere for Makes to run, no one for Makes to command, no one to fight and die for him. His actions and decision are now going to be punished!

The enemy makes their move and attacks. Makes takes every effort to bring down as many as he can; he stabs one and then another as he is able to kept them back for a minute. They are an overpowering, deadly force, and their deadly shanks are striking quickly, many hitting Makes over and over again in the face, chest and hands.

Now bleeding profusely, with painful stabs and cuts all over his body, he becomes weak and falls to his knees, slipping into an unconscious state. Makes starts to see people he killed in the past, life is flashing quickly by. He feels a succumbing feeling of pain that is seemingly going on for hours, but it's only seconds. Then it is black and has ended.

The blood drips of the shanks onto makes lifeless body and taking his final breath, the deadly reign of Makes is over. He wakes up and finds himself alone on a football field. It's very dark and very hot out. Players are coming out of the darkness, one then another, running by and bumping hard into Makes and telling him, "Let's go, you're receiving the punt!"

Makes does not know what the hell is going on, and he tries to remember how he even got here? He is in a weird state of mind. He looks at his clothing: he is wearing a red tattered football jersey but no pads, and he has a helmet in his hands. As crazy as it sounds, Makes does as the players say.

When he runs out on the field, all the players look normal, as if it was a normal football game, but it's dark and there is a thick fog on the field. He stands alone, looking up and waiting for the ball to be seen and come down. The lights get lighter now, and fog starts to clear away; Makes can see the football in the air as it quickly comes closer. He catches the football and begins to run with it! Running hard and fast, he sees some of the players coming fast out of the thick fog at him.

Makes is still in a delusional state of mind, but he moves fast, missing a couple tackles, and then finds himself facing off with a huge, dark, unimaginable creature. He has nowhere to go as this monster of a player is quickly approaching. "What is this fucking thing in front of me?" He watches as it comes fast and hard toward him, and then there is blackness.

He awakes, and a horrifying face looks down at him, its heated breath falling on Makes' face. It's very hard to breathe; he figures there must be a bunch of players piled high on him. Unable to move, he yells out, "Get the fuck off me!"

"Not yet, Makes—we have something special for you!" A large knife appears and starts to come closer to Makes' face. "It's time to carve, "heard over and over." Makes hears that and starts to try to move, but he can't. The knife is coming closer to his face, and he yells out, "What the fuck! Get the fuck off me! I'll have you killed! Do you know who I am?"

Makes hears an evil and deep voice, a voice unlike any he'd heard before. "You know who I am?" There are laughs coming from other players. Makes thinking this can't be happening. Then there is a hard, sharp pressure entering his face. Then deeper, the pain has started, and there is nothing that can be done about it. The feeling of being cut, Makes tried to move his head to get away, but it just makes the cuts deeper. Blood fills his mouth, and he tries to spit it out but can't.

Paralyzed and helpless! The knife starts to cut another part of his face cutting it like butter; it starts from the cheek and goes toward the eye. "Not the eyes," Makes says loudly. "Please no!" The blade is cutting deep and slow; salty, wet blood flowing down quickly fills Makes' mouth, causing him to choke. The blade makes it to the closed eye and begins cutting deep into the eye and then deeper, hitting sensitive nerves. Makes feels a painful pressure as it enters deep in the eye socket, there are loud contemptuous sounding laughs now coming from the players, the same laughs Makes used to give to his helpless victims.

Makes can't take it anymore; the pain is too horrific and overwhelming. He tries to breathe, but it is not possible, as the blood running down his throat causes him to choke and cuts off his air. He is forced to take this horrific abuse, given by these sick demonic looking creatures—who seem to be enjoying all of this! The pain is excruciating and so overwhelming that it causes Makes to go into convulsions as more hot blood fills deep in his throat and causes him to suffocate. In the quieting distance Makes hears, "Six more deaths!" As His body is shutting down, and blackness comes.

Makes is able to move now, and his heart is racing. It's very dark. He feels around: there are hot metal walls surrounding him. There is a small hole above with a little light coming through it, and now it is getting so hot. The heat is so excruciating.

Makes—screams out loud, "Where the fuck am I?" He starts to remember being in prison and fighting those rival gang members. Then he had that hellish dream of playing football and having his face being brutally carved open! Makes puts his hand to his face and can feel the open cuts all over his face; there is still wet blood coming from them. "What the fuck is going on! Get me out of this fucking place!" he wails as he bangs hard on the hot walls.

It starts to get hotter, and the walls start to quickly glow a bright red. The pain from Makes' face feels like being stuck with a million pins. His blackened, tattered clothes are starting to catch on fire, and there is no space to move. Everything touched becomes an unimaginable pain, and his fingers burn as they stick to the heated walls. His lungs are on fire, taking short breaths of horrific heated pain that quickly saps the life out of Makes. Death is here, squeezing tighter and tighter!

Makes can't fight it anymore, and the horrific pain ends. All is black! He wakes up in a dark cell on an uncomfortable, worn-out bed. It is a bed that Makes has woken up on so many times before on. He says, "Shit, it was all just a fucking dream!" and gives a thankful out loud laughter.

Looking around something doesn't feel right. He sits up and gets out of bed, looking out to an open cell door and onto a badly weathered metal balcony. There is nobody around, no noises, no lights, just burning torches here and there. He gets up and walks out onto the balcony. He looks into the neighboring cells, nothing! "There must be something down stairs. Why is there nobody here? What the fuck is going on?"

Walking cautiously down the stairs to the first level he hears banging noises coming from one of the rooms about twenty feet away. He follows the noise; it's coming from a dark locker room that Makes new all too well. Makes enters the pitch-black room and it seems like its

150 degrees in the room, Makes takes his hand and wipes the dripping sweat from his face. There is a light from the bottom of a closed door about fifteen feet away, it's the utility room he remembers. He walks quickly to the room and approaches the door, when there is a loud sound like a metal bar hitting the floor behind him.

Makes startles, quickly looking around into the darkness, and he says, "Who's fucking there? You'd better show yourself!" hoping no one is there. A sickening smell suddenly over whelms the area as A huge dark figure starts to slowly appear quietly out of the blackness and is now standing only a few feet in front of Makes. Makes can just barely see him and says, *"Who and what the fuck are you?"*

There is only a moment of silence. The large creature staring down at Makes smaller body then quickly attacks. Makes tries to defend himself, but it's too late, he feels a powerful crack to the side of his head.

He awakens on the ground, with his head in horrible pain. He takes a few seconds to get his composure back. The door with the light begins to open slowly. Makes is only a few feet away and starts to crawl for the lit room. This time he makes it to the door and enters. The light is coming from a small burning torch on the wall.

When he fully enters the room, he feels his aching head and then looks at his hand, noticing it is full of blood! A loud noise comes from the dark room that Makes just came from. He yells, "I'm going to kill you, whoever you fucking are!" no one fucks with Makes, He looks for a weapon and sees a piece of thick pipe on the floor.

He still feels a little wobbly, wiping the sweat and blood off his face—after a few seconds he is able to get his bearing and feels like someone is going to pay for that assault. He grabs the torch in one hand and the large pipe in the other and cautiously goes into the dark room. "Come out, you motherfucker!" He holds the pipe tightly, ready to strike at any movement.

The door slams shut behind Makes. He startles and looks back, seeing there is nothing there. He quietly mumbles to himself, "What the fuck is going on?" He brings the torch forward and sees something go around one of the lockers, but when he runs over to the locker, nothing is there! He walks around to the backside of the lockers, the torch brightening the area.

Three huge creatures are now visible as they quietly wait and stare at Makes. Each creature is holding a large knife that look like a prison shank. They have large yellow eyes, charred blackened colored skin, and horrifically scarred faces. They are wearing old worn orange colored prison uniforms and stand about seven feet tall, towering over Makes' small frame. There is a bad stench emanating from them, like a rotting corpse.

Makes knows better now so he strikes fast and first and without hesitating hits the closest creature in the side of the face, a hit that would crush the bones in a normal person's face, but nothing happens! The hard hit from the heavy steel pipe seemed to bounce off the demon of a man, causing it no pain. The creatures retaliate, wasting no time and begin to strike back viciously. Makes feels an unimaginable pain again and again, all over his body . . . and then it is over. He falls helplessly to the floor, and lies there motionless on his side as a large pool of blood surrounds his lifeless body. Standing over Makes are the three horrific looking creatures, blood dripping off their knives onto Makes body.

Curled on the floor and in a delusional state of mind, Makes hears their sickening laughter over and over again, and he starts to have flashbacks of when he and his gang attacked a helpless gang member while in a locker room in prison; that day they made an example out of that guy, who was an opposing gang member alone in the same locker room in which Makes now lay. "We bloodied him up bad! Shanked his bitch ass!" Makes had spoken in a hysterical and crazed manner.

He shakes his head and comes to, looking up and seeing the creatures are still there. "Stay the fuck away from me," he whimpers as he starts to try to crawl away. Following close are the three creatures. "I didn't do shit to you motherfuckers" they laugh at him and let Makes's crawl some more, leaving a—blood trail behind him.

He almost makes it to the door that he originally entered, when one creature jumps on top of his back and starts carving deep into his face, just like Makes used to like to do. Makes is helpless, and his blood curdling screams ring out. There is no one to hear or stop the brutality.

The creature digs harder into Makes' face, and Makes can feel the knife cutting into his tongue as his cheek is cut wide open. The creature says, "You like this shit, bitch? You need some more?" As it carves up more of his face and the pain and blood loss bring Makes to the point of blacking out. He hears, "Four more deaths, Makes, only four more!" All quickly fades to black.

He wakes in the darkness and it's that horrific smell again! Makes' heart races as he is still having flashes of being stabbed again and again with his face cut wide open. He holds his hands up to his face and then touches his body. He is covered with small cuts that are crusted with wet and dried blood! Makes reaches out into the darkness and hits the heated walls of the box. "Not this fucking place again! Get me out of here!" The box slowly begins to heat up and begins to glow red. Makes screams out as the pain starts to overcome his helpless body. "No—no! Please stop, not this again!"

Priest

An old priest is sitting up on his large bed, just waking up. He looks at himself from a large mirror that hangs on the wall. The mirror is showing his ninety-year-old, frail body.

He just celebrated his birthday a few days ago, and it took a lot of strength out of him. There was a large turnout for his surprise party. He is somewhat of a celebrity in the neighborhood and church, where he has conducted services for over fifty years. The community is his family, and many showed up to see him, possibly for the last time! Everyone was aware he was looking very frail and would not be around much longer.

Around the room there are pictures, one of the pope and others of different priests. There are statues of Jesus and crosses all around the room. He feels very weak today and knows his time is near. He has been sick and weak for a while now, and today, given his lack of energy, he accepts his fate that death will come soon. He says a long prayer and then lies back onto the bed, taking his last breath and dying alone and a peaceful death.

He awakens in a concussed state of mind to a dark room to what seems to be a burnt out church. He can see his surroundings only through a small hole. He is standing in the dark, small room, behind a wall of some sort. He remembers he had said his final prayers and though he had died, maybe this was a dream and he has not passed yet.

He slowly starts to remember this place—over the years he spent many times in a place like this, as he continues to look through the small hole.

Why is everything old and in ruins? Then something catches his eye: it's a little boy about nine years old, walking by the front of the door.

The child walks out of his sight. He continues looking through the hole, curious and wondering if he should get out of this dark room, when the young child appears again, this time stopping in front of the door; he's holding hands with another boy. The priest starts to recognize both these boys. He feels around the room, realizing it is his secret place where he would bring his special kids.

"This can't be happening!" He looks back out the hole at both the kids, who are now looking and pointing at the secret door, pointing to wear the priest is hiding. More kids start to come, three, four, five of them. He looks at their faces and recognizes all of them, now feeling a sense of shame and helplessness.

Looking closer at the children, he realizes they are not ordinary. Their eyes are blackened, and some have their mouths open, showing their little sharp teeth; their nails are long and sharp. They begin to come closer to the door and begin to pry at the door. There is no place to run to for safety, nobody to call for help to stop this. He looks through the hole again, there are so many now!

The kids are wasting no time, they begin tearing and pounding at the door, and after a few minutes one kid's hands makes it through the frail door, and then another hand. There is no mercy in these kids; they seem to be out for revenge. The priest speaks up as the opening in the door is enough for the kids to start to come in. "Stop, I am a priest and you shall obey me!" But the kids do not stop. They continue tearing away the door more fiercely.

Let me wake up from this bad dream, the priest yells out, but it continues. As the door is quickly devoured, the priest backs himself into a corner, praying for the kids to leave, but his words are not heard.

The kids now are through the door, looking at the helpless old man that is curled helplessly in the corner. They walk closer and stand over the crying priest. They begin a horrific attack, striking with quick slashes from their sharp nails. The priest tries to resist the painful attack, but as he tries some of the children begin biting at his hands. He realizes there is nothing he can do to defend himself he is helpless!

He is scratched and bitten in the children's frenzied attack; blood spews out from all over his body. He lies now in a large pool of blood and is unable to move, barely alive. He is able to let out only a few helpless cries to "*Please stop*!" Over and over again he says, but there is no stopping them; they continue to attack harder and now with more anger.

The kids finally stop and then begin to chant over the priest's soft cries: "You will suffer and die many deaths here! You have six more, six more!" The priest hears the chant over and over again as he gets very weak and then takes his final breath. Blackness comes to him.

He awakens into blackness, trying to push away as if he is still being slashed by the kids. He quickly realizes no one is slashing or biting him now. "It's over! It was just a horrible dream. But where am I now?" It's so hot, and his body is in a terrible sweat. He feels around in the dark. There are thick hot metal walls all around him. The smell is horrible; smelling like burnt flesh. "What kind of place is this? Am I still having a bad dream?"

The body is in a horrible amount of pain, so he must be awake! There is dried blood and deep scratch marks all over as he feels his face and body—he realizes that it wasn't a dream. He sees there is a small hole in the center of the box, with a little light coming through it. He moves some of the thick ash that's covering up the hole with his finger, and then he looks out to the sight of more darkness, there is some light coming from somewhere out there.

He moves some more of the thick ash. He can see out now, and there is a blackened figure of something or someone out there! It's looking down at him and looking at it longer it looks like a large black fog with reddened eyes, just hovering there. Behind it there appear rows of large, blackened boxes. His finger penetrates through some more of the ash to see more, and then whatever it was, is now gone.

The box starts to become hotter as the walls are glowing red, like an oven heating up. The skin on his body is in an agony of debilitating pain as it heats more. Some parts of his clothes catch on fire, and there is no space to move and no way to get out; everything being touched burns in an explosion of horrendous pain. His lungs are filled with thick smoke and are burning to an unimaginable state as he tries to breathe.

Parts of the body are now on fire and death is here! It has surrounded him as it is squeezes him tighter and tighter, sucking the last bit of life out of him. Yelling out with great effort for this to please stop. Then as he can't fight anymore, there is no more pain; all the pain is gone, and all is black.

He awakens, his heart racing a million miles an hour. He tries to get focused, but the heart is racing too fast and slowly he realizes he's in another place and is able to calm down from that horrific dream. He looks around and remembers this part of the church: it was the sleeping quarters, off limits to only the priests, or so they said!

He realizes that this is his old room, but it looks a hundred years older and is much more worn. Finally fully calming his self he notices He's dressed in formal pajamas but is barefoot, and he begins to hear loud noises coming from inside the closet. The doors of the closet suddenly begin to shake as someone tries to get out.

He stares at the door, in a frozen state of mind and doesn't want to open the door because he fears what's inside. Terrified and with a feeling of helplessness he gets up and runs quickly out of the room and down a long hallway. There are small torches on the walls giving off some light. He comes to a set of closed doors and tries to open them, but they are locked. He hears something and looks back: there is a shadow coming down the curved hallway, and then more shadows are starting to appear!

He's afraid to look down the hall, but he has to see what it could be. By moving to the center of the hall, he is now able to look at who or what it could be, There are kids of all ages, from seven to fifteen, and they're dressed in their church clothes and are walking straight toward him. There must be twenty or more, and they keep approaching. He panics and tries again to open the door, but it won't budge. He looks back, and the kids are not far from him. He kicks the door and pulls the handle hard, frantically screaming out for it to please open but nothing opens it. The groups of kids are now only a few feet away, and they are holding knives and are ready to strike the helpless priest. Feeling an overwhelming sense of fear, he has no choice but to curl up on the floor next to the locked door, praying this will all go away.

There are tears filling his eyes as he awaits the deadly attack, and without looking he feels the first knife slice his hand, then another piercing the rib area. Excruciating pain enters his legs and then the stomach area, and he tries to scream out for them to please stop. But they don't stop, and loud evil laughter from the children is the only response to his painful cries.

After a few minutes of this horrific slaughter, the stabbing finally stops. The priest looks back, scared at what he may see, but all the children are now gone! Thank god he says out loud as he is lying helpless in a large pool of his warm blood, trying to move, thinking he must crawl back to his room. Every inch taken brings his body ever more terrible pain as blood seeps out of every wound.

He stops struggling and lies in the middle of the hall, fully exhausted and unable to go any further; any movement is overwhelmingly painful. The priest can hear footsteps now coming from down the hall. He looks up It's a boy who looks about fourteen with fresh blood on his white dress shirt, and he's holding a large knife. The boy reaches the curled up bloody priest, stands over him and softly whispers, "I can help end your pain."

"I'm okay, boy, please leave me alone. You kids are very evil and have done enough!" The boy holds up the large filet knife, and the priest says with what strength he can muster, "I said to leave me alone! You kids will pay for what you have done today!"

The boy quickly replies with a half smile, "No, sir, it's *your* turn to pay for all that you've done!" The boy comes closer, his eyes are evil and black and as the knife comes toward his heart, the boy begins chanting in a rhythmic voice, "Four more deaths to go, four more to go!"

The priest is in such pain and is so weak that he can't stop the knife, the knife inches closer and the chanting is getting louder, as the knife begins entering his chest. Blackness comes quickly.

He awakens and holds his chest, breathing hard. The thick smoke and heat immediately overcome the priest. He pushes out into the darkness and sees the small ached over hole. He realizes he is back in that box, and he cries out loudly, "Please let me out, I can't take it—not this again!"

Rapist Killer

Cutter sits motionless on the edge of a large, bloody bed in a quiet house in the upstairs bedroom. A body lies motionless on the floor, brutally beaten and blood all over her. Cutter is still, his eyes closed and calm. He takes in what has just taken place, humming to himself to relax his racing heart.

He is dressed in black clothing, with ripped marks on his long sleeve shirt and bloody scratches on his face. He is holding a large bloody knife as he gets up and walks slowly into the bathroom, he is exhausted trying to calm his breath, trying to relax his racing heart. He says to himself, "That was a good one," and he smiles as he looks at himself in the bathroom mirror. He sees the scratches and blood on his face. "Damn bitch gave a good fight!"

He flashes back to the woman and her desperate screams for help, trying to escape the protruding knife that kept piercing her once beautiful face and body, and then as she was raped over and over again. She loved it, she couldn't get enough he thinks to himself! He had a big smile as he washed the blood off his hands and then his face. He returns to the room, and there is already the smell of fresh death coming from it; it was a room where hours of brutality and torture had just taken place.

Someone is heard outside the bedroom door, and then the door of the room swings open, almost flying off its hinges. Guns are drawn—it's the police! Someone must have heard the screams coming out of the house, and called the cops. I knew I should have had that bitch gagged the whole time, though a little noise brings some excitement to the party and heightens the moment, he thought to himself.

Two police officers with their guns drawn look on in shock and horror at what they have came upon. Cutter wasting no time, turns and runs to make an escape out of the bathroom window, realizing there is no chance to get out. The police come closer to the bathroom, speaking loudly with a hatred in their voice, "Get on the ground!" Cutter remembers there is still a knife on the bathroom sink, and he is not going to be taken in without a fight. He reaches over and grabs for the knife, then runs toward the readied officers.

Shots ring out, and Cutter falls back like a car has just hit him. A thick black fog instantly appears and looks down at Cutter as he lies there motionless. Red piercing eyes look down into Cutter's eyes.

He takes his last breath like he is a fish out of water. He stares up at this black fog and knows this thing it's staring down at him, and all is quickly fading black. Cutter awakes, startled. His heart is beating hard as he remembers the police firing at him. He looks around at where he is and realizes he is in a prison. "What the fuck, where am I?"

It is a large and dark cell. He tries to walk but realizes he is sitting. He looks down, he's in a wheelchair!

There are large group of people sitting with their heads down. As he sits in his wheel chair, he wonders, "Where the fuck am I? How the fuck did I get here, and now I'm in a fucking wheel chair?" He remembers back to that nice blood bath, and then the cops showing up and firing their weapons. A smile appears. "They must not have killed the Cutter!"

The prisoners start to notice Cutter, and some turn and face him. Two large prisoners get up and start to walk over. Cutter realizing they are walking toward him, He tries to wheel away, but it's not possible, there's nowhere to go! They stand around Cutter for a moment, silent as if they are studying him and then begin to kick hard at his wheelchair, using their legs to stop him from trying to leave.

"*Get the fuck out of my way, bitches*!" Cutter says angrily, but the large men do not say anything back. One punches Cutter in the side of the face, and then the other hits Cutter so hard it knocks him over and out of his wheelchair. Now the whole cell begins to chant loudly and beat and kick Cutter brutally.

Lying there helpless, trying to cover his face and body up from the hard hits he is receiving, Cutter almost goes into an unconscious state with every hit. He feels his face and body start to swell. One of the men speaks loudly in a hard, deep devilish voice, "We have our new bitch, boys!" There are laughs heard all around.

Cutter is unable to move and is positioned faced down. He hears uncontrollable laughter and sickened words coming from all around him. "You're going to like this, bitch! "Then they begin to brutally rape him. While this is happening others continue to kick him hard in the head as they chant, "Six more deaths, Cutter, only six more deaths," as Cutter goes unconscious.

Cutter yells out into the blackness, remembering being in that horrific cell with those hellish creatures. He realizes it is over. "Must have been a bad dream!" He pushes out into the darkness only to hit the hard and hot steel walls. He screams for someone to help. "What is this fucking place? Someone get me the fuck out of here!"

He lies there for a minute, looking into blackness and smelling that horrible stench of a smell, like burnt bodies. He remembers the smell! Cutter burned a few bodies in the past, and it's something that will always stay with him.

The walls start to glow red as the tiny room heats up. Cutter screams out in horrific pain as his skin and his clothes start to burn. There is no space to move, to get out! The horrifying fear of burning alive is realized. Death is here, burning the life out of him. He can't fight the pain anymore; the pain has finally gone away, and everything has gone black.

He awakens sitting on a bed, trying to catch his breath. He realizes now that he is out of that horrifying firebox, and he calms down, he begins to recognize the room. He has been here before, even killed here before. He remembers it is that woman's house! It's dark in here, but he is able to still see enough of the surroundings.

There is a light coming from the room across the hall. He gets up and walks quietly over to the room, cautiously entering and looking to see whether someone is in there.

There is someone and it is a woman, and she is on her knees as if she is praying. She is wearing bloody blue jeans and a black bra. He walks closer as if he is in a trance and remembers a day he had a woman locked in this very room, for days. She senses you are in the room and looks back, and the door slams shut. Her piercing black eyes and scarred face is staring back at him. He goes for the door, but the door is locked and won't open. Cutter turns slowly back at her, a chill comes over him and she is still on her knees facing the wall, but still looking back at him. He searches for another way to get out, sees there is a window, and slowly goes to it, but it won't open. Then he looks back at the woman again, and she is gone!

Cutter looks around franticly, heart now racing and then notices that she is behind him and now she is holding a large knife. He recognizes the knife immediately: it's the same one he used to use on all his victims. Her face is badly scarred and cut up, her eyes are blackened, and there is no emotion showing on her face. It's horrifying! As she stares back into his eyes, paralyzing his next move—the knife is held high, ready to strike at any moment.

She begins her massacre and starts to stab hard at Cutters face. The penetrations are excruciatingly painful as blood flows fast. He tries to grab the knife to take it away, but the blade is so sharp that it cuts deep into his fingers, almost cutting them off. The strikes have left his bloody face and now have gone to his chest, one after another, causing him to fall helplessly to the ground. She stands over his now bloody body, her knife still thirsty for more she is not done with him yet!

He holds his bloody wounds and tries to tell her to please stop as she brings the knife closer, hot blood dripping onto his butchered face. She begins to strike again, this time penetrating deep into the stomach, and the pain is horrific as she moves the blade to the left then to the right!

He curls up and screams out; blood spews through both hands as he tries to stop the pain and bleeding, hoping that the brutality will finally stop, screaming out for her to please stop, but it doesn't help. The knife comes closer to his face, and he turns his head away to keep the knife from cutting more. There is a deep, slow cut that comes to the side of the face, and tears from his wet bloody eyes pour down his cheek. He can't control his breathing, and the pain is so terrible; he just hopes that at any moment the brutality will end.

He tries to yell out, but only helpless and bloody mumbles come out. He feels the pressure of her knee hold him down causing excruciating pain and blood to spurt out of the open holes. Then he feels a sharp pain to the groin area, and there is a feeling of being instantly sick, causing him to throw up. She begins to speak loudly—but he cannot understand her. He looks up with his cloudy blood stained eyes, trying to focus on her seeing that she is still holding the knife and holding something else bloody in her other hand.

Darkness comes in and out, "Four more deaths, Cutter, you have four more!" Then all goes black. He awakens into darkness, and it's so hot! He's startled and feels as if he is still in that terrifying room, still trying to get away.

He feels his face and then he feels down for his genitals and says, "What a horrific dream!" He reaches out into the blackness only to hit the hot metal walls. He remembers this box as it begins to heat up and the walls start to turn a glowing red. He screams, "No, please no! Not this again, I can't take this anymore!"

Suicide Bomber

There is a group of men huddled in a small mosque. They have their special meeting today, and everyone has to be there. It's Ali's big day today, the day he will meet his seven virgin wives. It's to be an honor and celebration for him and for the group. There have been many protests in the streets, and Ali is chosen to make those sinners pay today. These kinds of actions are not tolerated, and this organization will be the ones to make the example.

The leader says, "Ali, it's your time today, brother!" A cheer is heard from the others members as they bring a large vest and put it on Ali. Ali is only twenty; these members have been Ali's family since he was twelve. Ali's uncle brought him into this organization to fight off the infidels, and also to fight the Muslim sinners who were fighting with the infidels.

At age twelve Ali was on the streets as a lookout for this organization; later at thirteen, he would run weapons, and this organization took good care of him for it. Ali was fed well; they gave him money and treated him like a man at such a young age. When Ali was fourteen, his family found out what he was doing and tried to get Ali to stop and leave the extreme organization.

His family told him the things he was doing and the people he was with were bad. Ali didn't fully realize what his actions were; he was still young and looked up to his organization, because they were real men who fought for a true cause. How would Ali know about what his actions have truly done? He was a young man and knew that war was all around him, who were the good and who were the bad?

When the organization took Ali in, they said they were the good guys; it was in their religion to be fighters and stop all opposing evil forces! "We fight for a true cause, Ali, and your family should honor us, respect us!"

Later that week a bomb went off at Ali's house, killing Ali's father and his sisters and everyone in the house next door. Ali's mother and his little brother came out alive, and they immediately left and went into hiding, abandoning Ali. His mother thought Ali and his organization made their decision. The organization told Ali that it was the infidels who did this. "That is why you must fight with us, Ali!" With nowhere to go, Ali had his new family and would do anything to keep it that way.

"Your time to commit to the family has come, Ali. We need you. You will be blessed for your good today!" After strapping on his vest, he puts on a loose-fitting robe. Ali isn't scared; he has waited his whole life for an honor like this. "*I am very proud today*," Ali says as he hugs the leader.

"You will do good for the family, Ali. Others have gone before you, and your new wives are looking down at you right now, waiting for you." Ali smiles as the leader continues. "You know what to do, right, Ali?" The leader grabs Ali hard by the arm, and there is no more nice talk—it's all serious now. Three men check the vest. "Ali, this is what you pull. Once you pull it, you have three seconds. You know where the location to pull it is, we went over it many times: right in the middle of the market. Right, Ali?"

Ali replies in confidence, "Yes, I know! All those sinners will pay today!" Ali finishes getting dressed and is led to the door. "*Look normal, Ali,*" he hears as he looks out to the crowded street. "*You are a hero today*". He walks out to the crowded street and starts to blend in.

A large market is five blocks away. Ali walks quickly, thinking the whole way about the new life he will have with his beautiful virgin wives, and how he will make his family proud. He walks to the area chosen to set off the bomb; it is very crowded, but he pays no attention to the people, the only attention is to the vest, and without hesitation he pulls the fuse.

The three seconds are like slow motion. Ali looks around looking at faces of families, grandfathers, kids. It's like Ali can see them all, but like they are all looking at him! Then it's over, and there is blackness.

It's a beautiful palace. Standing alone in the middle of the room is Ali, and he looks around and sees no one. Ali is wearing the clothes he had on that day. Something goes by the bedroom doorway, and Ali gets excited and says loudly, "Yes, I am here. This is my palace now. My wives, I am here, I have made my journey!" He has a large smile on his face.

Ali walks out to the living room and sees the backside of a woman in a beautiful burka; she is staring at something outside on the balcony.

Ali walks slowly, excited. "I have done it—this is the greatest feeling ever in my life."

He reaches out to grab the woman and says, "*You are my wife to obey me forever. Turn around, my love.*" He looks at her now face to face; she is wearing a veil, and nothing of her face is showing. He lifts up the veil slowly, and as her face is revealed, Ali can't believe the sight of the woman. Her face is scarred and old, and she still has her eyes closed.

He looks away from her for a second and stares out to a darkened view of a city. It is a horrific, dark underworld of some kind; thick layers of smoke hover over everything, with some sort of blackened boxes that float around the city.

Ali is in denial, as if this is a bad dream. He lets the woman go and turns to run back to the bedroom. He makes it to the bedroom door, stops, and looks back to see the woman starting to come toward him. Ali yells loud at her "go away," and he closes the door quickly and locks it before she can get to it. He tries to hide his disbelief and can't believe what is happening. His heart is racing, saying, "Where am I? How could this be?"

Ali turns to look around the room. There is another wife lying on the bed, dressed in her beautiful clothing. He doesn't know what to do and looks franticly around the room for another way out, but there isn't one. When he looks back to the bed, the woman is gone! The door flies open, and one by one his seven wives enter the room.

They're dressed beautifully, each wearing a different color burka. They enter and huddle together in front of the door. Ali is in disbelief; here are all his beautiful wives, but something is terribly wrong.

He has nowhere to go; the entrance is blocked, and he is forced into a corner as they approach. All the wives are now showing their hands, which are holding large stones. As they get close to Ali, they raise their arms, ready to strike. "No, stop this!" Ali's words don't mean anything as they begin to hit him.

He tries to defend himself but can't, he feels his fingers breaking as they are hit, then his arms, and then many strikes come to the face and head until Ali lies there brutally beaten and barely alive.

Ali hears one woman speak softly, "Your wives are here not for your pleasure, Ali, but to make sure your deaths are horrific. You have made wrong choices in your previous life, and now you will begin to pay for your sins. You will die here many times, all horrible deaths. You have six more deaths, Ali." While she talks, Ali hears laughter coming from the other wives as they continue to beat him. Ali taking his last few breaths and hears no more.

He awakens into darkness; it's very hot and smells horrible. He reaches out and finds only hot metal walls around him. "It's so small. Where am I? Let me out of here!" Ali screams. "Do you hear me?" He is still in a panicky state of mind.

Now the walls start to glow red, and it gets hotter. The skin on Ali's face and body blisters, it's so excruciating. It's hard to breathe, and a helpless feeling comes as panic sets in. Parts of the clothing that Ali is wearing catch on fire as the box becomes unimaginably hot. There is no space to move, no way to get out and everything burns in excoriating pain! Ali begins to pass out, and the pain is gone, all is black.

He awakens and stands in one of the palaces rooms, letting out screams as if he is still in the box being burning to death. Ali is in a kitchen area of the palace. He regains his composure back and looks around. He notices there is a window and quickly goes over to it; it has a view of a darkened street. He runs to the door, not wanting to stay in the palace. "I'm not staying in here again! I remember this horrific place!" He looks around warily for his wives as he bolts out the door and into the dark street.

The street is torn up, like there has been an earthquake or something. Nothing is living here but evil darkness. There are some torches that are lit on old worn out street poles about every fifty feet. Ali looks around as he stands cautiously in the middle of the street, and then he sees a group of people in the distance walking together. "*Who are these people?*" he says quietly to himself, and he tries to hide behind some rubble.

The group is coming in Ali's direction and they are walking slowly. Ali sees one in the crowd with some sort of a vest, like the one he had worn before. The group's clothing looks all tattered and torn. It's the same people that were in the market when Ali pulled the timer on his vest. These were the people he had blown up! Ali is horrified and can't believe this is happening. "It wasn't supposed to be like this!" He starts running away from them.

After running down one street and turning down a long alley, he reaches a dead end. Ali is stopped by a high metal fence that has a metal door in the middle of it, but it won't open. Ali goes to run back the way he just came, but it's too late as the group of the walking dead is coming! They are walking faster now that they see Ali. His heart is racing out of control as he cries out, "This can't be! Let me wake up out of this horrible nightmare."

They are now only ten feet from Ali, and he realizes he is trapped. Franticly he tries one more time to try to open the door, but it won't budge. He is now surrounded with nowhere to run. He sees that the person who is wearing the suicide vest is now standing in front of the group of people. Ali screams, "Get away!" He knows that it may blow at any second.

Ali has nowhere to go. He curls up in the corner, hoping that all this will just go away. A few seconds later Ali feels the pressure of being grabbed by many hands and hit hard all over his body. "No, please no! Get away!" he cries out hoping for them to stop, and then it stops.

Ali looks up, and there is no one around! Only the vest is there, a few feet away. He tries to get up and run away, but he can't because something is holding him back! He goes to move his arm but is unable to; there is a thick chain wrapped around it attached to the fence.

Ali starts to hear voices coming from the darkness of the alley: "You will die here, Ali!" Ali covers his ears, trying to stop from hearing the evil voices that are now ringing inside his ears. He looks around and tries to look for something that can break the chain, but there is nothing! He stares back at the vest and screams, "Why? Why is this happening to me? Let me go!" "four more deaths," the crowd chants.

Ali is totally exhausted and his arm is hurting him bad, maybe he pulled it out of the socket from trying to get away. He sits silently and stares at the vest, trying to catch his breath, it's too much to take in. The chanting gets louder and faster. There is a loud crash that comes from behind Ali on the other side of the fence, and he covers his face, thinking it is the bomb going off.

He looks back at the vest, realizing his helpless fate, and the chanting gets faster and louder. Ali eyes are growing bigger. "Just blow up already!" he says angrily as if the bomb can hear him. Then a huge pressure hits, and all goes black! He wakes up in darkness, kicking around and grabbing his face and body, saying, "I'm alive! I'm alive!"

It's so hot, and the smell is horrific. Ash hovers in the air so thick that it's hard to breathe. Ali now realizes where he is and says, "Not again, no please! Someone get me out of here!" He starts to bang on the walls, and the walls begin to heat and glow red.

CHAPTER III

WILL GOOD TRIUMPH OVER EVIL?

The Gang Leader—Makes

A meeting is being held in a large field at one of the deadliest prison in the United States. Five of the top gang leaders are there. Makes is one of them and has the top gang in the prison. After the meeting he returns to his cell with his top leaders. Makes gets ready to give his men orders his decision determines if there will be war with the other gangs, or if there will be a truce and peace.

He stands over his men, who are sitting quietly in the cell, waiting for the orders to be given. He thinks on the answer that was given so fast last time, without the need to think it out. The answer that would give pain and death to so many! Makes looks around at his men, who give their full attention. Many look crazy almost like animals. They're living in this prison, ready to kill at any moment for the gang. As Makes stands ready to give the final orders, there is a different feeling inside of him, a strange feeling he is not used to that causes him to shake his head, as if it will help with his decision.

Looking into the eyes of his battle ready men, he says with a confident voice, "There will be no war, there will be a truce!" One of his men quickly stands up and loudly says, "No! There must be war; we need to take them all out now while they are scared and unorganized! And if you don't have the balls to start it, Makes, then I will do it."

Makes looks at his disobedient soldier with an evil stare and said in an angry but steady voice "no one talks above Makes." "Makes, is the one to make all decisions." The soldier was Makes number two. Makes realizes where he is coming from; many painful and brutal deaths have accrued here, in this very unholy prison. But things will be different now! Change has to come and peace will be made.

Makes comes toward the defiant soldier, who stands and tries to stand his ground. Makes has to make an example out of him, he knows what he must do. He rapidly takes his knife out of his sleeve as he comes to him, and in a split second he begins to stab fast and hard, directed right to the throat. As he strikes, he releases all the pent up rage that has been building inside of him as he kills his own soldier. The soldier falls bloody and lifeless to the floor with his head barely attached.

Makes says again, "*I said there will be peace!*" He looks around at his guys, and they are undisturbed by the bloody body lying at his feet. Makes looks around and into the eyes of his men and says loudly, "Do you understand me?" And they reply, "Yes, we do!" Makes says "Good then, it shall be!"

The Priest

The priest wakes up and sits on the side of the bed. He looks in the mirror; he looks to be in his mid thirties. Getting dressed into his new cassock, he feels happy that today is a very special day. Today will be his third service as a priest, and something very special will also happen today.

He finishes up and goes downstairs, ready for his Sunday mass. It's early, and the service doesn't start for another hour.

One of the younger altar boys is there sitting waiting patiently in the front seat by himself; he was requested to get there early. The priest looking at the boy and is very happy that he is there. As he passes by the secret room and, takes a moment to stare at it, there is an inner, powerful feeling that comes over him, a feeling of righteousness to clear any evil thoughts he was having., He looks at the large cross hanging then back at the secret room, and he feels something deep inside; he doesn't really know what it is and where it came from, but it is strong enough that he knows that no bad things will happen today!

As he approaches the innocent young boy who is sitting patiently awaiting the priest's words, all the special thoughts he had planned for this morning have gone away. Clearing his distraught dry voice, he says to the awaiting altar boy, "You kids who all help with the church are all little angels! If there is anything bad that happens to you that you can't tell anybody about, you can always come to me, and I will make sure you will always be safe. Never will you be in harm's way as long as I am alive!"

The Rapist Killer

A man named Michael drives around an upscale neighborhood just outside of Chicago, having done so a couple times before, and he notices all the single woman as they get off the train and walk home. It's a good place to do some evil today! He says under his breath in a sadistic tone.

The thought of committing a sick and heinous crime is here, but when is it going to be? Will it be today? Michaels prying eyes catch a beautiful woman walking by herself, knowing that there is an alley only two blocks away, and she is walking that way. "This must be the time, I'm ready!" Happily speaking out as he grips the steering wheel tighter. He looks down at the large knife on the seat and a black ski mask that's ready to be used. "Once she makes it to the alley that will be the time!"

Driving slow as she gets closer; only a half a block more, up ahead there seems to be a small problem: A lady with a kid is having a problem with two troublesome looking guys. He comes up to the lady having the problem, and her back is turned, but the daughter looks like it's his niece. He slows and looks closer, and the woman turns. "*It is my sister*! And it's her little girl standing there with her."

Losing whatever thought of the harm that was going to happen to that walking woman, he pulls over as these men begin to get physical. He grabs the large knife on the seat, coming at them with it in his hand. The two men notice and immediately run away. He checks to make sure his sister and niece are okay, and they are. He escorts them to his car.

When he gets back into the car and drives away, he asks his sister in an angry voice "What are you doing over here?" She says with some panic still in her voice, "We got off at the wrong train stop and since it was a nice day we decided just to walk home. Lucky you came by, big brother!" She smiles, reaches over, and gives him a long hug.

Michael drives another block and sees the lady he was following earlier; she is now holding a small child, and her husband is there with her in front of a house. Inside a huge feeling of righteousness overcomes him, and he looks down, grabbing the black ski mask, and throws it out the window, never again he says under his breath.

The Suicide Bomber

Ali is being strapped into his vest, which is filled with explosives. He then leaves the warehouse and walks through the crowd to make it to the designated location.

He doesn't feeling very confident today, even though it's a great honor to the group and to him, and to his God for his special sacrifice. He walks quickly but notices that there are children and families casually strolling by, they are all unaware of the special sacrifice today.

He arrives at the spot and has a very uneasy feeling in his stomach. He takes a quick moment to look around and again notices all the people that are in the market. Looking closer and on the other side of the market, a group of men are talking with each other. Ali sees someone in his family, it is his mom and little brother!

Ali can't believe it and is so happy; he hasn't seen his mom in seven years, and this is a very special day! They don't notice Ali; they are at the market buying some fruit the same market that Ali is supposed to detonate with his vest.

Ali looks around at all the innocent people and says, "I can't do this, not to my family or any others!" He turns around and walks quickly back to the people who are making him do this horrible act. Ali instantly starts to get yelled at, one even hits him hard in the back of the head. Any disobedience is punishable by death.

Ali says loudly, "It's not me! It's the vest! It failed. I was there in the spot, and I pulled the timer three times, and nothing, it didn't work!" Ali begins to take off the vest, and members of the group come over, many looking angry with Ali. Ali drops the vest carefully and says, "I need to get some fresh air, I'm exhausted." He begins to walk away from the group toward the door. Ali looks back as he walks faster and sees that they are foolishly playing with the vest, and one pulls on the timer. In an instant the vest blows up.

The explosion instantly kills everyone in the building and destroys much of the warehouse, Ali is only a few feet from the door when it goes off, and with his momentum going toward the door, he is blown out to the middle of the street and is covered in flames. People from outside hurry and smother Ali, and the flames go out. Ali looks at his tattered and burned clothes. He is partially burned, but he will live.

The End

An Empowered Legacy

Story I: Grand Island Palace Casino

Story II: Anna's Empowered Legacy

Part 1:
Grand Island Palace Casino

Log Line: Play your cards right on Grand Island . . . or your last hand dealt may be your last!

Synopsis: The stakes are high when the Grand Island Casino approaches fifteen professional card players with the chance of a lifetime: A five-day private Texas hold 'em tournament held on a private island with luxury, fine entertainment, and the opportunity to win a twenty-five million dollar cash prize.

Both card skills and survival skills will be tested as players are challenged to advance by winning their daily Texas hold 'em tables, thus ensuring their exemption from a night of survival deep within the darkness of island jungle, where they will not be alone!

CHAPTER 1

THE NEW BEGINNING

As I entered the ballroom, I was greeted by a tall beautiful Spanish woman who looked like she just came from a model's runway in Paris. She began to inform me about the ballroom. "The drinks, food, and women are all compliments of the tournament." I couldn't help but smile as I looked around the room at all the beautiful women. I thought this was a dream come true, but a chill ran down my body as I started looking around and thinking, "This is too good to be true . . . and what's going to be the real catch of this 'special' card tournament?"

Ray It's a hot, mid-afternoon summer day in Las Vegas, and unknown as yet to Ray this will begin the journey that will haunt him for the rest of his life. He is standing alone while in a long registration line, waiting to sign up for a big Texas hold 'em tournament for this weekend. He looks around at some of the competition and thinks, "The competition doesn't look too bad. It's mostly amateurs, so I should do well."

The line is moving very slowly, and it's getting very hot outside; the registration table is only a few more minutes away. Ray thinks, "Finally. Then I can go inside, enjoy some air conditioning, and get in a few hands of blackjack and a few stiff whiskeys."

Only five more players were left to register. Ray stands with his arms crossed, tapping his foot. He can't wait to get out of this line. He's startled when there is a tap on his shoulder. It's an older man who seems to have come out of nowhere. Ray gives the older man a quick once over and is impressed that he is dressed in such a high-quality black suit. Ray immediately thinks it must be one of the owners of the casino.

The older man leans in and asks, "Ray, can I please have a quick moment to introduce myself?" and he begins to pull Ray in closer to him. Without giving Ray a chance to speak, the older man says in a serious tone, "I have been sent to invite you to a private Texas hold 'em tournament, with a winner-take-all prize of twenty-five million dollars. You will have the honor to be playing against some of the best card players in the world! It would be the tournament's pleasure to have you accompany us at this private gathering. The tournament is to be held on a private island in a beautiful mansion. There will be luxury, woman, and much more. Everything is paid for, compliments of the private tournament!"

The man in black then asks Ray, "Ray, are you interested in coming to this private tournament?"

The man in black looks around for a few seconds and realizes Ray is next in line to sign in for this tournament. He stares at Ray, seemingly impatient. "Sorry, Ray, but I will need your answer quickly."

Ray looks down, thinking of the money and the private Island for this tournament. He thinks, "It sounds like a great time! And at least it will get me out of this hot desert." He then asks the man in black, "When is the tournament going to start?"

The man replies, "Your plane will be leaving later this afternoon."

"What about an entry fee?"

The man in black replies with a grin, "This is a very special tournament, and the man who is hosting this special event is taking care of everything; all that is needed are the players."

Feeling confident and lucky, Ray says, "Why not, yeah, I'll do it!" The man dressed in black, replies with a happy grin, "Ray, you will be very pleased. You have made the right decision." He pulls Ray off to the side and out of line. Ray gives a gesture with his hand to the sign-up table, as if to say he will not be signing in. The man in black says, "Go home now, and in your mail box, there will be a packet. In that packet will be your plane ticket and the necessary information you will need for the tournament."

The man in black shakes Rays hand, and Ray instantly feels the man's hand is cool; there is an uneasy feeling as Ray looks into the man's dark eyes, but he is interrupted when the man replies loudly, "Good luck, Ray!" before leaving.

As he walks away, Ray thinks, "All this time waiting in that damn registration line. Why couldn't he have found me earlier!" He heads quickly to his car. "I hope this was not a bad joke, but that man did seem very professional. But how did he know my name and where I live?" Once in his car he drives quickly to his house and arrives fifteen minutes later, immediately going to the mailbox. There is a packet, just as the man in black promised.

He goes inside the house and opens the large burgundy packet. In large letters written at the top is, "For Ray's Eyes Only." Written underneath that are instructions: "Go to the Las Vegas airport with clothing for seven days, and use this airplane ticket. When you have arrived at your final destination, someone will be there to take you to a designated hotel and check you into your room. Wait for further instructions. If you are not there on time to turn this invitation in, you will have then forfeited your chance to participate in the tournament."

"This seems to be easy enough," he says as he gathers his things quickly and leaves for the airport. He parks his car in the extended parking area and starts to make his way inside the airport. He's not familiar with this airline, because all that's is on the ticket is a gate number. He asks an airport employee where is this gate, and the employee says to Ray very politely, "You must be VIP, because you're in the private sector of the airport, and you will be flying on a private jet today."

Fifteen minutes later he arrives at the gate, surprised that there is a private plane waiting for him. He asks the lady at the check-in booth, "Is this my gate?" He shows her the ticket and notes, "It doesn't say where my destination is!" The assistant said, "Yes, sir, this is your flight, and I'm sorry, but the destination of the flight is undisclosed."

After boarding a short time later, Ray gets settled into his seat, realizing he is the only one on the jet besides a nice looking Spanish stewardess. The jet is high luxury and makes Ray feel like a VIP. The stewardess says, "Hello, Ray, welcome. I'm sorry, but under the tournament's requirements I am going to need to take your cell phone and your watch, please. You will receive your phone and watch back afterward."

Ray looks at her like this is a joke; it's very strange to be asked for these items. But she is serious, and Ray gives them to her without any problems. The stewardess says, "Thank you, sir. Please sit back and enjoy the flight! Would you like a whiskey or something to drink?" He thinks, "Yes, give me a bottle!" But he decides to be polite and only asks for a glass of whiskey. "Light ice, please; I like my drinks stiff. Thank you."

The flight takes off, and after ten minutes he asks the stewardess for another whiskey drink. He finishes his second glass and now feels tired; it has already been a long day. He thinks, "I'd better try to get some sleep."

The stewardess wakes him hours later as they get ready to land. Ray looks out the window at a small airport that seems to be located in a tropical country. The plane stops while still on the runway, and the door opens as stairs are quickly brought to the door. Ray jokes to the stewardess, "This must be my stop," and he gathers his things. "Good-bye and thank you." He walks out of the door to a warm, slightly humid day; it looks like the sun will be setting soon.

On the runway, a large, stocky, well-dressed Russian introduces himself as Leon. "Mr. Ray, Welcome. I hope you had a nice flight. I am here to escort you to the hotel." Leon takes the luggage from Ray, and they walk together toward two large white vans that are idling and waiting.

Leon hands the luggage to one of the drivers of the van, and Ray and Leon get in the other van. The vehicles drive out of an open gate. Ray asks in a joking voice, "Leon, where are we? Or better yet, what country am I in?" Leon answered him in a thick Russian accent, "I'm not supposed to talk about any details, just bring you to the hotel." Ray smirks. "Then Leon, I'm ready for you to take me there."

After a short drive through the thick jungle, they arrive at the hotel. They get out of the van and take a quick look around, stretching for a minute and embracing the warm tropical breeze; the temperature is around seventy-five degrees. The hotel is a nice, medium-sized, upscale hotel, with a colorful tropical landscaping. Ray says to Leon, "Now this is what I'm talking about! Very nice!"

He takes his luggage from Leon and says good-bye before walking into the hotel. He is met by another beautiful Spanish woman. The hostess says, "Welcome to our hotel, Ray. I hope you will enjoy your stay with us." She gives Ray a key to his room and says, "Your in room 220 and it's up the stairs."

Ray walks up to the room and opens the door to a very upscale, tropical styled room. He immediately smells the fresh flowers that are on the dresser. After looking around he says, "Very nice." But he notices the room has no TV or phone, just a king-size bed and a fully stocked wet bar.

He settles in and has a couple drinks before lying down and nodding off. Then a large envelope is slipped under the door. He is startled awake and his heart starts to beat faster as he wonders what to expect. He reaches down and picks it up. The envelope is a large burgundy one with Ray's name written on it in big letters. He opens the envelope, and there is a large invitation letter that has a signature standing out at the bottom by someone calling himself The Man.

> Ray, welcome! Soon you will have the pleasure to play in my very exclusive private tournament. All that is needed now from you is to sign and put this invitation in a box that is located at the far end of the hall. In the morning when you check out, you will receive another envelope; in that envelope will be your instructions to meet at a certain place in the morning not far from your hotel.

Ray is awakened the next morning by a soft knock on the door. He is lying in his comfortable bed, rubbing his tired eyes, taking in the fresh breeze and the sound of chirping birds coming from the open window. He still feels tired from the jet lag, and also from not having a good nights sleep. All night he tossed and turned, thinking of this private tournament.

After packing up and having the breakfast that is offered, it is time to check out, and as expected an envelope is waiting for him there.

Inside the envelope are directions to a boat dock. Before walking out the hotel door, he pauses for a quick moment and thinks, "This is it, this is the start of my new adventure!" Ray laughs quietly to himself and thinks, "How do I get myself into these things?" Then he steps out of the hotel to a beautiful, warm, sunny day.

He follows the directions and looks around as he walks. There seems to be no one else around. He follows an old sidewalk that zigzags through the rainforest, and then he comes up to an old brick street that leads down to a small boat dock, where there are about ten people waiting. There is also a large white luxury yacht, and two gorgeous Latin women stand in front of it, dressed in short white dresses; they seem to be the hostesses.

After ten minutes of waiting, one of the hostesses speaks up. "Welcome! It's now time to board." They direct everyone to go down into the bottom area of the yacht. When everyone gets settled in, one of the women tells everyone, "Please relax and get comfortable. Drinks will be served shortly."

Ray looks around the cabin area: it's set up very classy and is nicely decorated, with a poker theme. There is wrap-around seating and two nice leather couches located in the middle of the room. The cabin windows are tinted black so that no one can look out of them; nobody is allowed to have watches, so there is no way of seeing how long of a boat ride it is going to be, or what is even around them.

Ray sees some familiar faces and recognizes almost everyone. He can't believe the competition, these are some of the best players in Vegas, and in the world! The yacht gets under way, and everyone holds up their drinking glasses and gives a cheer: "To the tournament!" A few drinks later, the yacht docks, and everyone is escorted off onto the dock, standing around and needing a minute to fully take in this beautiful tropical island.

A large white mansion stands in the distance, and the hostesses say with big smiles on their faces, "Follow us, please." Everyone stays in a group and walks toward the mansion. They see some of the most unique and beautiful tropical gardens they have ever seen.

CHAPTER 2

THE MANSION

The fifteen of us now gathered at the front door of the mansion and then entered through the large front doors. As we walked in, we immediately noticed the huge, beautiful room, which had a painted cathedral ceiling and early 1900s décor; it was very unique and classy!

Then all eyes went to four beautiful women that were standing there waiting off to the side. One spoke up. "Hello, gentlemen, and welcome to the mansion. We will be your tour guides to show you around the mansion and then to your rooms."

I couldn't believe it! These were some of most beautiful women and high-class settings I had ever seen. These women each looked like they were models, and each one seemed to be from a different country. It was a very welcoming sight, to say the least. Everyone's attention was on the women, and we were escorted around the mansion and then settled into our rooms.

My hostess informed me, "The mansion will be hosting a very special welcome party for all the players. It will be starting at eight tonight, and the party will last through the next day. The tournament will start on the afternoon of the third day. You are free to relax and enjoy yourself in whatever way you'd like." As I walked into my new room, it was a beautifully styled Venetian themed room with fresh flowers on the dresser and a large, stocked wet bar, but again the room had no phone or TV. After taking a hot shower and getting settled into the room a bit, I couldn't wait to go downstairs to the bar area for a couple of stiff whiskeys.

On my way down, there was a huge crystal chandelier that stood out in the center of the ballroom that must have cost a small fortune. The ballroom was a 1940s design, and it had beautiful redwood on the walls and a high-vaulted, hand-painted sky blue ceiling. Whoever designed this ballroom did not spare any expense. A large, tropical bar was set off in the back of the ballroom, and was occupied by many beautiful and well-dressed women of different nationalities.

I finished walking down the long spiral stairway and officially entered the ballroom. Standing there waiting for me was a beautiful Latina wearing a big smile, and she began to inform me about the ballroom. "Welcome, sir! My name is Isabella, and I am the hostess for the ballroom. If you are in need of anything or have any questions, please feel free to ask me—The drinks, food, and women are all compliments of the mansion." I immediately had a big grin on my face as I looked around at all the beautiful ladies. This was a dream come true! But a chill ran down my body again for the second time as I started looking around, thinking, "Maybe this is too good to be true. What's going to be the catch of this tournament?"

The party was a big success, and everyone was laughing, having a great time, enjoying the company of the beautiful woman. The party was interrupted briefly when two of the players got into a very loud argument with each other.

One was a big, stocky guy who had his hand bandaged up and was missing a finger. Everyone wondered what his story was but didn't dare ask. He had a crazy look and feel about him. He was a big man, mostly muscle, and looked like he should be doing security or something, but poker brought in all kinds. Later I met a guy named Bill. He and I were sharing a similar interest, in the same women! We bumped into each other as we both approached her, and neither of us talked to her for now, instead striking up our own conversation.

We started talking, and I said, "Your name is Bill? I have seen you before; it must have been at one of the tournaments." Bill replied, "Maybe. I've been to a lot of tournaments, but nothing comes to mind where we've met before." Maybe I'd just seen Bill on TV before. We began to talk more about our pasts and where we were from, and if either one knew what to expect in this tournament.

Bill mentioned to me that he heard something about tournaments that were being held on a private island, but he was unsure if this one was the same one. I asked Bill, "What things did you hear?" But Bill didn't answer and quickly changed the subject to the beautiful woman that was standing next to us. I didn't ask Bill anything further about the tournament, because the woman standing next to us had a beautiful friend that was in need of my attention.

The days flew by, and what a great time everyone had. We'd all have some great stories to talk about. But now it was the day of the tournament. At 2:30 everyone gathered in the tournament room. Now it was time to forget the past and concentrate on this Texas hold 'em tournament, and win some money!

We all gathered around one of the tables and were about to receive the tournament rules. There was some tension in the air as the rules were read. A very sexy hostess began to speak from behind the poker table. ***"Welcome everyone; I hope you have been enjoying your time here at the mansion."***

A player said loudly, "Yes, we have!" and there was some laughter from the others.

The hostess continued.

> You are here to play this tournament, which will be played here daily for the next five days. Your goal is simple: to win your table!
>
> As you all know, your competition is some of the best in the world, and if you are one of the lucky players to win at your table, you will be exempt from the night's activities and will be free to use all of the mansion's amenities.
>
> Unfortunately, if you are not one of the winners of your table, then the next game you will be playing will be a game of chance! You will be escorted out of the mansion at dusk tonight, and you will return only when the sun begins to rise. When you are outside of the mansion, there are one of our six deadly creatures you might have to face in the night. Six cards will be placed on this table, and one of the cards will be turned over each night. That will be the creature you might have to face! When you leave the mansion, you will be in

> the isolated back part of the island. Your goal is simple: to survive the night!

Players started to talk loudly and out of control to each other. The hostess spoke up. "Pay attention, please! This will be read only once!"

> You will be able to choose one weapon from our weapons room, which may or may not help you. When it comes time to choose, choose your weapon wisely!
>
> You are safe only when the sun comes up, and that is when the mansion door will be unlocked to let you back in. Once you return to the mansion, you will then be safe and free to enjoy the amenities of the mansion, until the start of the next game. Also, there is an outside boundary area. You will know when you come to it, it's a 15 foot-high, 220-volt electrified fence. Don't touch it!
>
> On the fifth day of the tournament, those who are left will be at the final table. If you lose to the other players or to The Man, there will be a boat waiting on the other side of the island for you. You will have to get to it to get off the island, and that will be the only time the electric fence will be turned off. But, you will have to face one or all of the six deadly creatures that will be waiting out there for you.
>
> If you are able to beat the players and The Man, then the money will be here waiting for you, and you will exit out the front door and be taken safely off the island.
>
> Gentlemen, you have come for the twenty-five-million-dollar prize, and you have accepted this tournament, so please play to the best of your abilities and walk out as the winner. It's now 3:00 p.m, and it's time to start the tournament! There are four card tables, with four players at every table except one, which has three. The names for the seating are on top of the tables. Good luck to everyone!

CHAPTER 3

CHARACTERS FOR THE FIVE DAYS

Ray (Main Character)

Ray was thirty-seven and was from a small town in southern Indiana. He stood at six foot one and kept in good shape. He was clean cut and dressed nice, and he was somewhat known as a ladies' man.

He sat thinking about being on this little private island owned by some crazed billionaire calling himself The Man. He was waiting for life to finish at any moment, on top of this high spot on the mountain on this warm night, and he wondered if this tournament was going to be the last one.

He'd grown up with a good family and two brothers in a middle-class family. He worked different odd jobs until the one day he found an opportunity to get out of that small Indiana town. Ray found a good job on the Internet: working in a casino in Las Vegas. The job was only a waiter's position at an upscale restaurant, which would be great money and would be a great change of pace; especially from the small-town living that he had been accustomed to all his life.

He moved and worked in Las Vegas, seeing all the people who had made all this money from gambling. Ray looked into gambling and how the poker games were being played. He met one friend, named

Joey D, who was working in the restaurant with him and was into the gambling scene, doing some bookie work and poker tournaments.

At the age of thirty-three, when he started to follow Joey D around and learned the ropes of gambling and some of the secrets that went along with it, like when to bet at the right time, how much money one should play, and when the player might be bluffing. Ray took special interest in learning all this. He wanted to be the best, and later one of the famous and rich, respected people in the restaurant, the ones he was always waiting on.

He started to play poker twice a week in the smaller tournaments, and in six months he was starting to do very well, winning one tournament every month. After a year of doing this and starting to get into the bigger tournaments, he even started to get a ranking within a year and won twenty-five to forty thousand dollars per game. Ray was quickly on his way in the gambling scene.

Six months later, Ray won it big, taking a big prize of $150,000. Ray's life changed fast after that. Now he was able to live it up a little, and he loved Texas hold 'em, which he now made it into a full-time job.

Bill

Bill stood at six foot three and had a muscular build. He kept in good shape, even after leaving the military, where he was in a special operations group. Bill had blond hair and kept it a little longer than his military days, along with a little facial hair.

Bill liked to travel, and with no wife and kids, he was just out to live life wherever it took him. He grew up in the big city and did not really get into the gambling scene until the age of twenty-five, after leaving the military. When Bill got out of the military, he was looking for something fun to get into, and after a trip to Las Vegas, poker was what he wanted to do.

Bill was very good at cards, and he played all the time. He was a natural and loved playing cards, and he quickly started to make a name for himself in the Vegas scene, doing very good at local tournaments. At the age of thirty-two, he won his first big poker tournament, winning a large pot of one hundred thousand. He later stuck around and winning a little here and there till his luck started to fade away, he decided to try a new popular game called Texas Hold 'Em. Bill caught on very fast and started to like the game even more than poker.

Bill concentrated hard and learned every aspect of the game, becoming a very detailed player who watched the faces and movements of all the players. He learned how to read everyone's face and actions, which was why he rose to be one of the top ten players in the Vegas scene in just over a year.

He was doing well for himself, living the high life in an upscale part of Vegas, when out of nowhere, he was contacted by a CIA recruitment agent. While he was in the military, Bill had worked with some of these agents before, and he had put an application in with them when he got out of the military, but there had been no contact with the CIA till now!

The CIA had told Bill that he would need to do their training, but during his training period he would have to continue his poker tournaments. The CIA said they would give Bill a full briefing after he had graduated from his training. Bill was very happy he'd always wanted to join this specialized group, and the fact that it was mandatory to keep up on the Texas hold 'em was even better!

One day when Bill was in line to sign up for a tournament, he was approached by an older man dressed in black. The man offered Bill what he'd been waiting for all his life: a huge payout tournament of twenty-five million dollars. It was music to Bill's ears, just to hear this amount of tournament winnings and better yet, it was winner take all.

The man in black talked of a special location on a private island and said that this was going to be a private tournament. To Bill the money was everything. It was the sort of prize where he would be set for the rest of his life, and it was a chance of a lifetime. Bill knew it, and he was going to take it!

Crazy Mike

Crazy Mike was a big Irish-Italian man that stood around six foot one and three hundred pounds. He wasn't all muscle, but Mike went to the gym almost every day and was very strong, working out like a power lifter. Mike always wore very nice clothing, and he favored dark suits by Armani. Mike had dark black hair that he wore somewhat long and slicked back, gangster style.

Mike was best known as a card player and thug. He grew up in Las Vegas on the rougher side of town and was into a little bit of everything. His real story began at the age of twenty-four, when he was offered a bookie job for some mobsters. He made some good money as a bookie, making bets for the wannabes of Vegas and doing some of the collecting when he had to. It was definitely Mike's kind of work. Mike especially liked collecting because it kept him up on the craziness of the business.

Crazy Mike lived it up in Vegas; he had a lot of money and women, and he enjoyed the nicer things Vegas had to offer. Then at the age of twenty-six, Mike started to get into gambling at a professional level, but his main job was still to keep up with the bosses' needs.

A lot of Mike's time was spent around high-class mobsters and their friends. Mike wanted one day to follow in their footsteps. He started to do his own private bets on the boxing fights in Vegas, which he was good at predicting, and he won a lot of money on the side. He had a great time keeping up with the company of his mobster friends till that unfortunate day that eventually came to all gamblers of Las Vegas, which Mike had seen too many times before!

Mike got greedy and made a very large bet, and unfortunately he lost. He'd had some inside information and thought his bet was going to be a sure thing. He thought of crazier schemes and became more panicky, wanting to win his money back, and not in one month but now! Mike thought that asking to borrow money from his mob buddies was going to be the simple thing to do. Why not? For Mike those were his brothers, the Goodfellas as he liked to call them.

Inside their office were three high-class mobsters. They were sitting around in leather chairs and couches, smoking large cigars. One of them, named Big Tony, sat at the small bar set in the back of the room, and he looked almost bigger than the bar.

Mike asked, "Can I have a minute of your time? I need to borrow some money and put it on a sure thing I have." Mike quickly added, "I'm good for it."

Mike had worked for and was friends with many of these guys for years. The head mob guy in the group, named Crazy Joe, reclined in his leather chair with his cigar held loosely in his hand, and he said, "You know it's not good doing business with friends, Mikey. It's never good." The two others quickly agreed with Crazy Joe.

Mike pleaded, "Only this one time, guys." Crazy Joe had an angry look on his face. "Mike, we all know you're good for it, you work for us." The other guys laughed. "But remember, friends are friends till something happens, and we don't want this something to happen, do we, Mikey?"

Mike wanted to borrow one hundred thousand, and eventually the mobster guys gave him the money. He was grateful for getting the money and put it down on a big upcoming fight. He had gotten some insider information on this fight, and it was going to be a sure thing. He felt confident and thought, "It can't happen two times in a row. What are the odds of me losing again? I'm a professional."

The fight started to come around, and Mike was getting a little worried, wondering whether the risk was going to be worth it. Mike could easily give the money back and earn the money back he'd lost in a few months, and he'd be good.

He wanted to buy a new penthouse on the strip, and he was getting a great deal on it and needed the money for the down payment. "Yes, making this bet was worth it. Why fucking wait? I'll win my money back, get my new penthouse, and keep enjoying my upscale life, with no worries."

The day of the fight came, and Mike decided to watch it by himself in a quiet bar, located fifteen minutes outside of the Vegas strip, which was his private getaway spot. He sat down and ordered his favorite drink, a black Russian, and watched the fight.

The fight was going good, and Mike's fighter was really killing the guy, but things dramatically changed. His sure thing took a lucky shot to the chin and got knocked out in the middle of the fourth round.

He yelled out, "It wasn't even a punch, you fucking bum!" He sat there in total disbelief at what had just happened as well as the consequences that were going to come with it! Mike stared at the TV, watching the replay of his fighter getting knocked out. His face began turning bright red, and in one of his out-of-control adrenalin rages, he began to go crazy. Mike threw his half-filled drink at the TV and then began to tear up the unsuspecting bar. He threw chairs, punched a couple guys in the face, and even threw a guy over the bar, breaking half the bottles on the shelf. It was a very bad night for the people in the bar, talk about being in the wrong place at the wrong time!

He was awakened the next morning to the sound of the phone ringing. It was the call he knew was coming, his gut told him even before he answered it that it was his so-called brothers.

"Mikey," the voice said, "we told you it's bad business, this loaning money to a brother. We hate to take your money but you know the rules! It's business Mikey, so I guess we'll see you tomorrow".

After one day of no sleep and unsuccessfully trying to get some money, he had to tell the bosses the situation, thinking they would understand because they were "brothers" and all. He hoped that they would just give him some time to work it off, and he'd pay a little interest. But when Mike made the call, he heard the words from the bosses that he never thought he'd hear. "**Mike, you have three days, or you will get a visit!**"

Mike knew full well what the visit meant, he was the guy who liked paying other people visits!"

In a last desperate move, he took the last of his money, placed some bets on other events, lost, and went deeper into debt.

The third day came upon Mike, and sure enough he got a knock on the door, first thing in the morning.

Mike had known the four guys at the door for a very long time. They were now ordered to make an example out of Mike, and when Mike opened the door, they immediately started to rough him up, holding Mike down and with one cut taking Mike's left pinky. Then they started to leave. Mike looked down at his bloody hand and at his pinky lying on the floor with blood all over. One of the guys while leaving said to Mike, "Mike, we were told you have one week, or we'll have to bring the shovel."

Mike unfortunately knew what the shovel meant everyone, and it wasn't what he wanted to hear, especially when he had the never-ending desert surrounding him. Mike knew of a Texas hold 'em tournament that was going on in three days with a good pot. Somehow if he placed in the top three, he would have most of the money for the bosses and would make good for a payoff.

He'd played a lot of Texas hold 'em and tournaments over the years, and he liked the game. Mike was pretty good at it, winning some sometimes and placing in the top five a bunch of times. He was able to borrow the sign-up money for the buy-in but then a strange thing happened the day he was in the line to sign in for the tournament.

Mike was approached by a tall, older, well-dressed man in black, who offered what Mike thought was a joke. Mike instantly grabbed the guy by the throat and said, "If you're lying, I will break your fucking neck right now." Then he thought rationally for a second. "Oh my God! Maybe this a blessing in disguise, and I could get out of this fucking town and go to some beautiful island for a private tournament, with a twenty-five-million-dollar, winner-take-all prize!"

Mike let the guy go and fixed the man's wrinkled jacket, saying, "Sorry about that. There's all kinds of lunatics in Vegas, and I don't put up with anyone's shit. So, when do we go? I only need the plane ticket, and I'm on it." The man in black replied, "The information you need is waiting now for you in your mail box, and it's only for you, Mike. Good luck, sir!" And the man in black was off. Mike left the line and hurried home, and sure enough the information was waiting there in the mailbox when he got there.

He read the information and hurriedly packed a few things before grabbing his plane ticket and information and heading for the airport. When Mike parked his car in the airport garage, he was stopped, by two large men who had been following him. Mike knew the two guys very well. They stopped him, and one asked, "Where you going, Mikey?"

Just hearing those words come out of the mouth of his so-called friend was all it took for Mike! His blood started pumping, and the crazed rampage began. Without hesitation he began to beat the two guys half to death. Even with his missing pinky and in pain, he didn't care. Mike just beat the faces of the guys bloody, hearing the bones in their face cracking.

The two guys who had been given orders by the bosses to stop Mike at any cost from leaving Vegas now lay there in their own pool of blood and listened faintly to Mike's sarcastic voice. "I'm taking my four-fingered hand and leaving to a special place, so have fun with your fucked-up faces in fucking Vegas, and you can tell the bosses to shove whatever I owe them up their asses."

Without looking back, he checked in and got on his private plane. He was soon to be on an island, safe from his former brothers of Vegas. But unfortunately for Mike, safety would come at a price!

DAVE:

Dave was from Southern California. He grew up in the San Diego area, and now in his early twenties he was fully into the poker scene.

Dave was a fairly big guy at six feet and 220 pounds, and he wore his long brown hair in a ponytail and kept a long goatee. Dave's dad was a legendary professional poker player, and so was his Uncle Tom. While he was growing up, the family would gather up and travel to all parts of the world. It was very exciting, traveling to places most of his friends had never heard of.

As Dave grew up, he learned all aspects of the poker games, and was exposed to the true and professional gambling way of life. He grew to love the game of poker, especially Texas hold 'em, which fit Dave's style. He felt very comfortable and relaxed when he played. At the age of twenty-one he was old enough to make his move in the fast-paced Las Vegas scene, and he started playing in tournaments with his dad and uncle, as well as some Texas hold 'em tournaments by himself when he had the chance.

He did well at both games but shined even more in the hold 'em. It was his generation's game. At the age of twenty-two, he won a couple big tournaments for twenty-five to fifty thousand dollars, and he got rated as one of the youngest top-ten players in Vegas. Later, at the age of twenty-three, he won two big tournaments for $75,000 and $125,000. Dave was now a real contender, and he loved it!

One day as Dave was in line ready to sign up for a Texas hold 'em tournament in Vegas, he was approached by an older man dressed in black, who offered young Dave a chance at the biggest pot he had ever heard of. The only downfall was that the answer was needed immediately. Dave was told this special tournament was to be held on a private island with a lot of nice amenities—women, luxury, upscale accommodation, and much more, and it was all paid for by the tournament host. The man in black said, "Would you like to accept this once-in-a-lifetime opportunity?"

Dave thought for a second. I am young, and an offer like this would let me retire me very early. Like my father told me regarding gambling, 'Son, if you're going to do something, make sure as hell it will be worth it.' This would defiantly be worth it, especially if I were to win it!"

After a few minutes Dave said, “Yes! Yes, I will come to this tournament.” The man in black gave a large grin and said, “Wise decision, sir. Go to your mailbox, and the information you need will be waiting for you there. Do not tell anyone even your dad or uncle about this venture, or else your spot in this tournament is terminated.”

Dave complied and drove quickly home. Sure enough, the information was waiting for him. After reading the information, he felt happy and was ready to start the new adventure “For the first time there is something on my own! Without Dad or Uncle Tom!” He poured a couple shots of tequila and packed up a couple things. He took his information packet and plane ticket, and he was off to see what fate had in store for him.

CHAPTER 4

DAY ONE—LET'S START THE TOURNAMENT!

Ray "Welcome," a woman says. "It's time to start the tournament. Players, please take your assigned seats." As I walk toward the poker tables, there are four custom tables positioned in a circular pattern. Each table has its own unique style, detail, and wood with a special colored felt. The room's walls are made of beautifully colored dark wood with lots of custom molding, and on the ceilings there are large wooden beams going across.

The carpet is a deep reddish color, and overall the room is very classy and upscale. Someone has taken a lot of time, money, and effort to put together a unique poker room. I find my name and sit down at my assigned seat. I look down at the floor, and there is a custom emblem etched in the felt of each table: five cards, ace to ten, all spades.

On the walls there are some pictures of men whom I never seen before. One stands, a painting of an older general of some sort, with a style of uniform I don't recognize. There are three doors in this room, one where everyone has entered and two more toward the far back; I do not know where they lead.

The dealers are all women and are in sexy black uniforms with short skirts and high heels. Their hair is pulled back, and they all wear relaxing smiles on their face, like they have done this before. Everyone looks around, and some are asking where the host is. One of the staff speaks up. "Sorry, but The Man shows himself only at the final table. Please take your assigned seats, and good luck to everyone."

The cards are dealt, and the tournament has officially begun. I am feeling somewhat ready after trying to get my composure back from the past two days of fun debauchery and entertainment. The realization of being in this horrific tournament has set in. It's time to really try to focus on the card game, but with my mind racing, I have a rough time getting comfortable and concentrating.

The Texas hold 'em game has gone on now for over three hours, and the last player has finally gone out. One of the hostesses speaks up. "That's the end of day one's card tournament. Winners of your table, please go and relax, and enjoy yourselves with women, drinks, food, or whatever else you may desire." The winners are escorted out of the room by two very hot hostesses.

I had a terrible day. These players are all professional and very good, and I am escorted with the rest of the losers to the back area of the poker room. We all gather around a table and are given our instructions. The hostess says in a loud voice that echoes through the now silent room, "First, we will begin with the viewing of the overturned card. Then we will proceed to the weapons room, where you will pick your weapon of choice. After you all have your weapons, then you will be escorted out of the mansion."

Six large cards lay face down on the table—One person is picked by the hostess to turn a card over, and the player jokingly says, "Let's see the big, bad creature." A few players give a nervous chuckle.

The player picks the first card in the top row, and the hostess turns the card over and holds it up for everyone to see. The room goes silent, and everyone falls into a silent shock. The card displays a man dressed all in black, with old Vietnamese type clothing, wearing a black hockey mask to cover his face. The creature has what looks like a very large build to him, with glowing red eyes that are piercing through the eyeholes of his black mask. He is also carrying a large knife in each of his hands.

I say to myself, "Great! What did I get myself into?" I remember the big grin from the man dressed in black when I said I would come to this tournament. He knew what I was accepting, certain death!"

I look over at Bill, thinking to myself, "This must be the place Bill mentioned, when we first met. He said he'd heard something about these islands, and when I asked more about it, he quickly changed the subject." Bill knew more about this place, and I was going to question him about it later, in private.

We are escorted to a large, wooden door and are told by the hostess, "This is the weapons room. You are given the opportunity to defend yourselves with one weapon of your choice." The door is then opened to reveal a very striking, Asian-themed weapons room that is filled with everything I could think of, from shields and crossbows to all kinds of old and new swords, but there are no automatic weapons or guns. The hostess tells everyone, "Go pick your weapon."

After about thirty minutes everyone is satisfied with their weapons, and we are escorted to another wooden door ten feet away. The hostess says, "This is the exit door, out to the back part of the mansion."

CHAPTER 5

WELCOME TO THE FIRST NIGHT IN THE JUNGLE

The large door is made of some type of heavy wood and is reinforced with large pieces of thick metal. The door is pushed open by the hostess, who wears a concerned but steady smile on her face. As the door fully opens, we feel a breeze, and everyone stands ready but is waiting nervously for the final word to exit the mansion.

The hostess says loudly, "Everyone, it's now time to leave the mansion." We begin to head out the door in single file. One player is still standing inside, he has a look on his face that says, "I'm not going out there." The hostess speaks up again. "Everyone is to leave the mansion!" She stares at the player remaining behind.

As we all congregate outside, we look inside at the defiant player. I have to give him credit, he didn't want to go out and he was showing that something more is going to have to make him leave than just some hostess ordering it. He is holding the sword tightly in front of him with the blade facing down.

The player looks at us and then at the hostess, and he yells out, "Are you fucking crazy? I'm not going the fuck out there!" The hostess replies, "Sir, please, I'm giving you a final warning. You are to leave the mansion now." The player looks at her and says, "Fuck you! I'm not going out there!" He turns and walks quickly toward the door that leads to the front part of the mansion.

As soon as the defiant player gets close to the exit door, it flies open, and he is met by four large, military-looking guys wearing black ski masks and black camouflage military clothing and they're armed with assault rifles.

The player is standing only a few feet in front of the armed men; he isn't expecting to see these soldiers. None of us are, this is the first time we have seen anyone else other than the hostesses in the mansion.

The player looks at his sword and then looks back at their guns. I guess he's thinking "What are the odds? Go and leave out the back door with the other players and face that horrific creature, or try my luck with these masked men, and get out of this mansion." One thing I can say is that all of us players think alike, we think about the odds on everything we do!

We can hear one of the security guys say with a Russian accent, "You are to leave out the back door of the mansion and continue to play, or else." The player responds in a loud, defiant voice, "Or else what? Fuck off, I'm finished with this bullshit tournament, and I'm leaving, so get the fuck out of my way!" The security guy says loudly, "Player, there will be serious consequences for your actions if you don't go and rejoin the group. This will be your final warning!"

The player yells, "I'm not going out there!" He runs as if to strike at the security men with his sword.

The first security guy doesn't use his weapon, but he dodges a strike by the player. One other security guard effortlessly kicks the sword out of the player's hand, and another kicks the player's knee. The player fell face first to the floor while another immediately jumps on his back and puts a chokehold on him till he lies there motionless.

It's over in seconds. Two of the security guards take the player's limp body out of the front exit door. It looks like the player made it to where he wanted to go, but not the way he wanted. The hostess looks at us and says without showing any sympathy for what has just happened, "Show's over. Have a good night, players, and good luck! Remember; come back to this door only when the sun comes up. Only then will the door be opened to let you in."

One player jokingly says loudly, "Show's over, guys, so much for our VIP treatment." We all turn and look out into the dark jungle; the sun just finished setting. Everyone is looking around, getting their composure and getting together with the people that they trust. Some are saying, "Let's go in a big group for more defense." Some are heard saying, "Two or three is better; we'll be less of a target."

Then the giant wooden door slams shut behind us, and we hear it lock. We all turn, looking at the door. I think, "What a helpless feeling!" We hear a bolt lock, and then a giant latch crashes down. It sounds like the locks will stop a car if they have to. We all start to walk off into the jungle's darkness.

It is a nice night out, a little dampness in the air with a slightly cool breeze. As I look into the distance, there is only a little moonlight coming through the clouds, and it gives a reflection on the many large and big-leaved trees and plants. It's very dark in places, and the jungle is very quiet except for a few occasional noises from animals. Only a few lit paths stand out.

I partner up with Bill, and we both chose crossbows for our weapons. Some of the players run for distance from the other groups, and some are walking slower with caution, disappearing into the foliage.

Bill and I let the others go in front of us, and we venture to find our own area. After a twenty-minute walk, we find what seems to be a good spot. It's located on high ground, and it's possible to see the mansion and the entrance door. With the little light from the moon, we are able to see some of our surroundings. We sit and wait with our weapons at the ready. I think, "With us being somewhat close to the mansion, will this spot work? Or will we be the first to meet this horrific creature?"

We sit back to back and enjoy the breeze, watching what seems to be the only ways up to where we are positioned. I feel somewhat safe. Then I begin feeling nervous, It's the first time in my life I have to protect myself with a weapon.

Bill has some military experience that he talked a little about, and he can use a weapon if he needs, so I have confidence in being partnered with him. About thirty minutes go by, when there is light from the back door of the mansion. We can faintly see two large security guards dragging out the player that they detained earlier; his body is still limp.

As the player lies there lifeless, one security guy yells at him. "Wake up, asshole." It echoes through the silent jungle. The other security guy gives a hard kick to the player's ribs. Another security guard uses an air horn that he holds out of the door, as if signaling someone or something. After three long blows from the air horn, the two security guards hurry back inside the mansion, and the door closes.

We can see the player laying there for a about five minutes, and then he starts to come to, struggling to get up. From our view, it doesn't look like he has a weapon. The player makes it to his knees and tries to stand, but he looks to be in too much pain and ends up falling over and then curling up in a ball at the front of the mansion's door.

Soon after we can see something large coming out of the darkness of the jungle and walking straight toward the unsuspecting player, It is the huge creature and I can see its glowing red eyes and the huge swords it is carrying, looking like it came from the pit of hell.

The player must have passed out, because the creature walks right up to him and, with no hesitation, pokes him with one of his swords. The player starts to come to and must have woken in horror, looking up and seeing that horrific creature standing over him. "Get away from me!" His voice echoes through the dark jungle. The creature knows now that the player is alive, and it raises both of its swords, ready to strike.

The player is still in the fetal position, and he can only put his arm up to block the strike coming from the creature's sword. He lets out a horrifying scream as the sword strikes down and takes the player's arm off with ease. I watch and think, "This can't be happening!" The player tries to get up and make a run for it. He attempts to stand, but the creature swings again, striking the back of the player's leg and severing it like it was butter. The victim yells out for the creature to stop.

The creature stands over the player with his swords held over his head, waiting as if he is taunting the player. After ten seconds or more, blood is spewing everywhere as the player tries to helplessly crawl away. The waiting is then over as the creature gives the player a final blow, striking down effortlessly with both swords across the belly of its helpless victim, opening the player's belly wide open.

I can faintly hear as the player let out a few more quiet screams; then they stop. The player lay motionless, dead. The creature waits for a second and then turns and runs back into the jungle, disappearing into the darkness. I look at Bill, in horror at what just happened! I pray, "I hope we don't see this or any other creatures—and suffer the same fate."

After nearly five hours of waiting quietly, we hear more screams off in the distance, and after twenty seconds the jungle becomes silent again. I hope whoever the player was, he was able to get away or kill that thing that was after him. After waiting nervously for our own encounter, we finally see some light from the sun coming up, and Bill and I are relieved—but I wonder if the screams we heard earlier in the night means someone else is not coming back.

The mansion door is open now, and we are the first to make it to the large door. We look around the outside of the door, and I point and say to Bill, "Look over there." It's the player that we watched being killed last night; his body is all bloody and mangled under a thick bush, and his bloody limbs are in different places close by.

I'm feeling sick from looking at that hacked-up body, but I don't throw up. We enter the mansion, go to the weapons room, and turn in our weapons. When we leave the weapons room, I say to Bill, "See you for lunch." Bill replies, "Yeah, Ray, I'll see then." We head our separate ways.

I make it to my room and take a long, hot shower. I'm not very hungry and eat a few potato chips before trying to pass out. I lie there in bed thinking, "This has been a very exhausting and stressful night. I am beginning to think maybe I can't go through another night of this horror. Maybe if I lose again in the next game, I'll be the one unfortunate enough to meet one of these horrific creatures!"

I can't relax or sleep and I look at the mini bar in my room, thinking, "Now I see why we have a fully stocked bar in our rooms." I pour a shot of whiskey, then another. As I'm drinking, in the back of my mind I'm hoping my head will be okay for the tournament later this afternoon.

Chapter 6

Day Two

Day two of the tournament, and three days left. I wake up with a pounding headache, too much whiskey. After getting ready, I make my way down to the kitchen area for some lunch. As I arrive, I see players are gathered around the large kitchen table. Some are sitting and some are standing, and I can tell that something bad happened. Some are speaking in a panicky voice, talking about what happened last night and about the player who was killed.

The player talking was still in shock as he explained what happened. "That creature found our group last night. He stalked one of the players in our group, and then in an instant he dragged him away into the jungle's darkness. We could hear the player but couldn't see him, he was putting up a good fight with whatever that thing is, but after a few painful screams, we could hear he was no match for it, and it sounded like he died a horrible, painful death."

One player spoke up and said he was able to see the monster. "It was a terrifying sight, just like a monster you would see in a horror movie or at Halloween. This was a huge creature. It had red eyes that glowed out in the darkness, and it was holding two huge knives just like in the picture. The creature came silently out of the darkness in front of me and struck violently with both of its huge knives at my teammate. Then it grabbed him and took him into the darkness. It was showing no mercy, only seeking to kill!"

I didn't tell the group what we witnessed the creature do by the mansion door, but I said, "When we came in this morning by the mansion door, we saw the player that had been detained earlier by security. He was lying dead about ten feet outside of the mansion door, with his arm and leg cut off."

Everyone was silent. Two players were lost in the first night; thirteen men were left.

Day 2—Tournament

It's three in the afternoon, and everyone has gathered again in the poker room. It's now time to start the second day of the tournament. The hostess speaks loudly, "Players, please go to your tables and find your assigned seats." Everyone is quiet and looks nervous. You can really see it in everyone's eyes, the fear of losing today is not going to be an option! Nobody wants to see one of these monsters tonight. Today is a more serious game, and later there is a fight at one of the tables with that big guy with the four fingers. From what I could see, sitting from the next table over from them, the big guy named Mike lost all his chips and was out of the game. He went to get up and punched the guy that was sitting next to him in the face, breaking the guy's nose. The player had taken all of Mike's chips.

The poor player had to stay and play with his newly broken nose, because there was no stopping the game, and the hostess just gave him a towel for the blood.

I kept thinking, "Four days left. I'd better make every bet count." But it doesn't work to my favor, and I am quickly out with an all-in call that didn't go my way. I look over at Bill at the other table; he is out also, so tonight I'm praying not to see the creature.

Everyone has now finished with their games and it is the same setup from the night before. The three winners are escorted to their rooms and are very relieved. They are pumped up, yelling "Yeah! Thank God!" They call us losers and say, "Good luck, guys!" as they are escorted out of the room. Everyone gathers around the table where there are now five large cards laid out on the table. The hot Asian hostess is waiting for the card to be turned over; at least looking at her, it takes the edge off a little!

The last person that went out is picked to turn over the card. The card is turned over, and everyone looks for what type of creature it will be tonight. The hostess holds up the card, and everyone is silent and shocked by the looks of this creature. It seems to be the height of a fifteen-year-old kid, but it has a very heavy build and a dark colored face, as if he was black. He has red glowing eyes and wears somewhat tight-fitting black clothing that covers his whole body and the bottom part of his face. He is carrying a large knife that is similar to a machete.

The hostess speaks with a half of a smile. "You guys like what you see? Go now for your weapons at the weapons room—for tonight's game of death!" Bill and I look at each other. I say, "Game of death? She must be as sick as our host! She seems to be enjoying this." We pick our crossbows again, and as soon as the sun finishes setting, we are escorted out of the mansion.

This time there is no one making any opposition to leaving the mansion, and once we are all outside we hear the huge door shut and lock. I say to Bill, "This is really a horrible and helpless situation we're in. Some tournament."

The other groups head off and start disappearing into the night. We hang back and watch as everyone disappears, and we go for the same spot as last night. It's a good spot, located on the high ground, and we can hear if someone is coming, hopefully! There is also a trail where we can make some kind of an escape if we need to. Tonight is similar: nice weather and a little cloudy with some moonlight. We sit back to back and don't saying anything, trying to keep quiet and listen for any noises. Bill has his view and I have mine, and then out of nowhere, in the far, dark distance, we hear the screams of someone.

There is a sound in that person's voice that says they're in a tremendous amount of pain, but it sounds like the player is making a fight of it, or else the monster is torturing and playing with this guy, because he has not finished him for a fast kill. Bill looks over at me and says, "Make sure whatever you do, you stay alive as long as you can. Don't be a hero out here." He was whispering very quietly to me. "Can I trust you, Ray?" "Yeah, Bill, you can trust me. Why do you ask?"

Bill says very quietly, as if someone is listening way up here, "I am with an agency that has been trying to locate this place for many years. There was a scientist in the past that did many experiments on prisoners during the Vietnam war, and rumor has it that the same crazed scientist that made those experiments is now doing them today, turning soldiers into unstoppable creatures and selling them to private and government agencies for their own personal killing machines.

"There have been a number of agents who have been undercover, trying to find this place for years. The agency only recently learned that a card tournament was being played on an island in an undisclosed part of the world, and many poker players were reported missing. We had an agent that had taken a tournament like this almost a year and half a year ago . . . and was never heard from again."

When I was approached by the man in black and he made the offer to me to come to this tournament, the agency quickly arranged to put a GPS in my luggage. We didn't have much time to plan, and we feared we were being watched. When I arrived at the airport, I had given the stewardess my luggage and my watch; I didn't see my luggage till I arrived at the hotel. Somewhere between the airport and the hotel, they found my GPS. I had it hidden in my luggage and in my watch, but when I received my luggage, the liner was torn and my GPS was missing. I couldn't say anything as it might raise suspicion; it was disguised in a key chain, so maybe they took it on suspicion. I'm hoping they don't know what it was.

"I made the decision that instead of aborting the mission, I was going to play along and try to figure out how to report this to the agency somehow. I have to find a way to send a message or do something for the agency to find us and stop this horrific tournament and sick scientist, before anyone else gets killed."

Bill seems relieved to tell someone what's going on, and I'm glad it was me. I like Bill, and if I can help him in any way, I'm happy to. I turn and look up at the sky, saying a quick prayer to make it out of here safe.

Chapter 7

Crazy Mike's Night Out

Mike lost the card game and then picked out his weapon from the room before going out into the night. Mike was in an intense mood, thinking that maybe he'd like to see this creature of the night, and he would be happy to let out some aggression on it.

The player that had won the hand that took all Mike's chips had sent Mike to the weapons room, but that was okay for Mike! But then the player made a smart-ass comment. "Good luck tonight, Mikey." And he wiggled his pinky up in the air. "Who does this fucking guy think he is? He's lucky I didn't break his fucking face, like I did to my so-called brothers in Nevada."

Mike had gotten all coked up before going out tonight; it was offered to all the players if they wanted it, and Mike had taken full advantage, needing some pain relief for his hand. He was set for the night.

Mike and his group had been walking for nearly thirty minutes, and when they finally found a nice, dark spot to set up at, they made a close circle, sat, and began waiting. Mike had made no friends on the island so far, only sticking up for one player named Bob at the ballroom party, but the guys in the group wanted Mike with them because he was good protection against the monster, if they were to come across it.

Later in the night Mike could not keep quiet, needing to stuff his nose with another fix of cocaine. Mike knew everyone was getting worried with him making a lot of noise, but he didn't care. "Who the fuck are these guys!"

He lay there thinking, "This is one fucked up position to be in, going from crazy mobsters to crazy monsters. Who would fucking think to have a game like this and have people stupid enough to be here to play it? Money! That's what—people will do anything for fucking money! At least there's a chance to win a huge amount of it, more then what's going on in Vegas. If it is to be my fate to meet any of these monsters, then so be it!"

Mike did another bump of cocaine, and then as his watery eyes started to clear up, in the distance he saw there was something out there moving around! A small, dark figure with glowing eyes was coming right at Mike. Mike with his large sword held tight and ready, he stood up and said loudly, "Welcome to the party, you motherfucking monster! He ran toward it and struck at the creature, hitting it in the right side of the chest. The creature was seemingly unaffected by the attack and moved quickly to strike back, penetrating its sword deep into Mike's lower back, causing Mike to fall painfully to his knees.

Mike was in pain and slowly got up, but he was still ready to give the creature another strike with his sword. But it was too late—the creature moved in quickly and effortlessly struck Mike again, slicing deep across his back, opening his back wide open, sending the big man to his knees again.

The creature waited for a second, ready to strike again but waiting for Mike's next move, a few seconds later the creature made its move and came back toward Mike. Mike waited for the right time, and with all the energy he could muster, he let out a yell and lunged his body forward, both hands on the sword. With an overhead thrust, he caught the monster off guard and sliced it across its abdomen, cutting deep through the monster like butter. But it seemed to have no effect! The monster still was on his feet, wounded but not showing any sign of pain.

Mike fell face first on the ground, having no more energy. Using what strength he could muster, he turned himself over onto his back. He was only able to get up enough strength to let out a few painful screams, lying helpless and exhausted and bleeding profusely out of his wounds. Mike was in very bad shape, and he knew it!

He waited for the creature to come finish him off, but it didn't come.

Mike closed his eyes in terrible pain, and he could not move and could only feel the numbness begin to overtake his body. He tried to keep quiet, listening to the fate of maybe one or two other guys, but he couldn't be sure. He hoped that was the end of the creature that it had left him for dead. Then it began to rain. Mike felt warm drops starting to drip all over his face. He lay there for another minute and then opening his eyes and there was the creature, quietly standing there! That darkened face and those red, glowing eyes stared down at Mike as if it was examining him. It was the warm blood dripping down from this monster's face, not the rain that Mike had thought.

It started looking closer at Mike; those red, glowing eyes staring at him and its hot breath on his face as it came closer. Mike tried to turn away but couldn't move. He lay there helpless, waiting for the creature to finish him. A voice came out of the darkness from behind the creature. Mike tilted his head back and could see that it was a fellow player, Bob, and he couldn't believe he was standing there. Bob had his sword held high, ready to strike at the creature, and he said, "I'm here to help you, Mike!"

The creature turned to strike back at Bob, but Bob was ready and, with a hard and fast thrust of his sword, he took the creature's arm off almost at the shoulder. The creature let out a loud grunt it was finally hurt. It moved slowly away as it went to its knees, and Bob turned to look at Mike. "Are you okay?"

The creature however was just playing hurt and sensed a chance to strike back. It lunged back up and struck at Bob, catching Bob off guard. Bob tried to strike, but the creature's large machete struck first and penetrated deep into Bob's neck, the man gargling as he fell to his knees. Bob was trying to say something, but nothing was coming out, only blood and garbled mumbles. He fell over, dead!

The creature gave Mike a quick look and then grabbed its arm and retreated into the darkness. Lying there, in terrible pain, unable to get up, and bleeding in excruciating pain, Mike was barely alive, with no hope of making it back to the mansion by himself. The sun started to come up, and Mike heard someone talking, someone was coming! He let out a painful sounding "Help!" The group of players heard Mike's voice, and Mike heard them as they started coming toward him. Out of the thick jungle appeared a group of four guys, who stood around looking down at him. Mike said again, "Help me, guys!"

Mike recognized one of the guys; he had a bandage across his nose. It was the guy Mike had punched in the face. Mike heard the guy say, "Can you believe it? There's that piece of shit that hit me last night, Big Mike. You don't look so bad now, Mikey. Looks like that creature got the best of you. You pussy, better you than me."

One of the other guys said, "Look over here." It was Bob's dead body. "Shit, Bob took one to the jugular."

Bob was Mike's only friend, and they had made a pact to watch each other's back. Mike thought back to the ballroom party, when some of the guys where messing with Bob, making Bob the butt of their jokes. Some of the players knew Bob from when he'd lost a big tournament that was televised. Bob did not have the balls to call and go all in, when everyone watching on TV could see he had the winning hand. He ended up trying to safely slow play, and with that strategy, he lost the big tournament and was constantly criticized, being called "no balls Bob" from then on.

While in the ballroom, some of the players were drinking too much and started to make jokes at Bob. The best one was, "What do you call a player with no arms, no legs, and no balls? Bob!" and they all started laughing loudly.

Mike was standing next to Bob at the bar and started feeling sorry for the guy. Bob was a little man, around five foot eight and weighing about 160 pounds. Mike always had a soft spot for the weaker guy, and told a players to shut up and get the fuck out of here, or else.

The other player said, "Or else what?" Mike said loudly, "Or else I'll bite your fucking finger off, like this one," and he held up his wrapped hand with his missing pinky. The other players immediately left, looking at Mike like he was nuts. Bob said, "Thanks, Mike, but you didn't have to do that. Mike replied, "Fuck those guys."

Bob said, "If you ever need it, I'll have your back!" Mike looked over Bob's little body. "Yeah, that'll be the day!" Mike snapped back to the present upon hearing the players talk over him. The player with the bandage over his nose said, "Let's go, guys. We have to get back to the mansion." One of the others said, "Aren't we going to help Mike?"

The nose replied, "I'm not lugging that big, bloody piece of shit anywhere." He came back over to Mike. "But, I will help him out with one thing." He gave Mike a hard kick to the face, and blood poured out of Mike's nose. "Paybacks are a bitch."

Mike lay there helpless, watching as the other players laughed at him and disappeared back into the jungle. He tried to say something but choked on his own blood. As the pain started to numb his body, Mike knew it was his time to die. Never in his life had he felt this way; he was always the one to inflict the pain and torture onto others, and now he was going to die alone in a place where no one would miss him, the way Mike had given it to so many others!

Ray: Bill and I sit back to back, waiting for the sun to come up and feeling like we have been up here waiting for days, exhausted and tired. Finally the sun starts to come up, and we are safe again. "Thank God," I say, "and what a relief. It was another long night, and I'm feeling very worn out." Bill and I run for the mansion, and after turning in our weapons, we say our good-byes and go to our rooms.

Like the night before, I get to my room and take a hot shower, and then I grab a bottle of Jack and head down to the kitchen to get something to eat. After a couple of roast beef sandwiches and a couple stiff drinks, I get the energy to go to the ballroom. As soon as I walk in to the ballroom, I make eye contact with a beautiful, black-haired Asian woman named Asha. She is somewhat tall and has a very firm and hot body; she shows off her long legs with a short, sexy black dress. We enjoy a couple drinks, laugh, and talk a little, and then I think I would love to spend all day with this beautiful woman. But I need to get some sleep at some point, so we go to my room and enjoy some time together.

When she leaves, I lie there motionless in bed, truly exhausted. I think, "What a way to take my mind off this crazy situation I'm in, and what a better way to end the day! Time to try to get a few hours' sleep before the next tournament starts, hoping my luck is going to be good and I'll win my table today!"

CHAPTER 8

DAY THREE

I wake up feeling very tired but somewhat revived, and I get dressed and ready. I grab a bottle of Jack and go for lunch in the kitchen, pouring a stiff whiskey on the rocks, and then I make a few sandwiches and start to listen to the other players talking.

They said that three more players were killed in the night. One player had been killed by being ambushed in the darkness as they were walking, and two were able to put up a good fight when the creature found the spot where there group had been hiding.

The big four-fingered guy was one of the guys who put up a fight, and the second guy was named Bob. Those must have been the screams that Bill and I heard last night. That now leaves only ten players left. The game is getting ready to start, and we all gather at our designated tables and find our seats. Today I am concentrating and feeling good. I'm focused and ready to win my table!

One problem is that my friend Bill is at the same table, so if one of us wins, the other has to go out on his own. Tonight everything is falling into place, and I am doing great. As for my friend Bill, he is unfortunately having a bad night and is the first one out. I suggested to Bill to go with me to the ballroom this morning and take his mind off things. If he had come with, maybe he would have been calmed down and would have had some better luck at the table.

After I take the last player out, I look over at Bill and feel sorry for him, but I'm also very happy to finally win and to stay in tonight. I look at Bill and say, "Be safe tonight. Don't be a hero." The other two winners and I leave with the hostesses and go back to our rooms. I am hoping Bill will fare well in the night.

BILL

I set out into the night with a crossbow and a group of four other guys that I barely knew. Immediately after leaving the mansion, the group started tramping through the brush, trying to be quiet, but they were not. They sounded like a herd of elephants, and nothing was quiet about them! I didn't feel safe going into the night's jungle with these guys.

While walking, I thought back to my military days. When I was in this small unit. The small group was silent and deadly, able to flow like a snake through the night over whatever terrain was in front of them. We made no noise and were never seen by anyone; it was a powerful and confident feeling.

But now, being with these guys from the big cities who had no military experience and didn't know what the hell they were even doing, it made me very angry. After thirty minutes of trampling through the jungle, the group finally stopped and found a good spot under a large tree. Everyone made a close circle and put their backs against the tree, looking out into the darkness of the jungle and waiting for whatever tonight's horrific monster was going to be that had been selected to hunt them down.

We sat there, and I thought about was my new friend, Ray. I hoped he was living it up back at the mansion. I knew I would be! At least I felt secure going out in the night with Ray, and we had our own safe spot, but I didn't want to give it away to these jokers; I'd save it for just Ray and me.

The group of guys tried to keep quiet, but it was impossible. They had no discipline and needed to scratch their asses or whatever, making a lot of noise. I said to myself, "Just go on your own. It will be safer," but I decided to stay at the tree with this group. It was still better being with these guys if we encountered the creature.

It had not been two hours when we heard something moving around in the distance. The creature was so big that we could hear it walking. It was coming toward us, and come it did! It was the first time

I had seen a creature like this. Halloween had its days as people had dressed up as monsters, but who would have thought a huge, horrific creature would actually exist and we were here to be its prey!

The monster got a scent of us and came right for us; I was at the backside of the tree, looking around and watching, as two of the guys in our little group were the first to be at the creature's mercy.

The creature came at the two guys with a loud growl like a crazed animal, and it held its huge hatchet high, ready to slice anyone who stood in its way. It was a creature similar to the first night, but bigger and not wearing a mask. He was wearing different styled and colored military clothing, and he carried only one weapon. The creature's face was nothing like I'd ever seen before; he looked like his face was scarred up and had been badly mangled.

I watched as the first guy ducked the attack of the creature's hatchet and then struck the monster in the side with his sword. It gave me room to shoot, and without hesitation I shot five arrows in succession and hit the monster in its chest with each one. The creature, seeing where the arrows came from, stared at me with those glowing red eyes. It was injured, and I hoped it would die. I took off and started running down a dimly lit path, the opposite way of the monster, my heart racing a million miles an hour. I had to find a position where I could reload and take aim again.

I found that spot after a ten-minute run. I stopped and laid there under a large bush with big leaves, so it was good cover. I was quiet, my heart racing as I tried to catch my breath, and I hurried to reload my arrows. Then I aimed back down the path in the direction from where I had run and listened. I could hear some screams in the distance, and then mercifully they stopped, everything went completely silent!

I hoped everyone fared well and stayed alive. I was proud of those guys; they'd stood their ground and put up a good fight, and they didn't just run away . . . but maybe it was because they had no choice. I had to run away, to reload my crossbow. It took time, and if I were to have stayed there to do it, I would have been a sitting duck for the creature to come get me, and by the look in its eyes as I shot those arrows, I know he wanted me. I tried to get my mind focused for what was to come for the rest of the night, fearing I would meet this monstrous creature again.

I started to think of my life up to this day. What a crazy life it had been! From the military days to the CIA, and now this ungodly shit! When I got the first chance, I was contacting the agency and getting everyone out of here, and then they should nuke this terrible island.

I also wanted to win this tournament and get that money. I would retire and live quietly on some exotic island, with beautiful women all around me. I would also invite my new friend Ray to accompany me, if he made it out of here alive. He deserved it, he was one of the good guys. I was covered in dirt and cool damp leaves, and my nerves were running thin. Thank God the sun was starting to come up.

I stood up, brushed myself off, and ran to the mansion door. I turned my weapon in and then walked quickly up to my room and took a much-needed shower. I ate some chips and poured a full glass of the first alcohol I could grab. After relaxing a bit and two more glasses, I passed out, only waking when someone knocked hard on the door.

CHAPTER 9

DAY FOUR

Ray

I wake up very refreshed, which was much needed. I wonder if Bill fared well last night. I get ready and stop by the kitchen area, and then I go for Bill's room, knocking on his door and asking, "Bill, are you there? Are you okay?"

He answered the door, I was relieved to see and hear his voice. "I saw it, the creature. I fired my crossbow at it. It was scary as hell Ray, it was the nastiest creature I've seen yet! It looked like the first creature, but this one had military style clothes and had a face that was all mangled, and it carried a huge hatchet."

"I talked with some of the players, and they said the monster killed three people last night! One of the guys said it tortured and cut up the wounded guys; he said the screams were horrifying because they were still alive as the creature cut away. The other player said they tried to kill it but couldn't, and that they had to leave the wounded to the mercy of the creature."

Bill brings me inside his room and turns the water on high to muffle what he is as going to say to me. I hope that it is good news, that Bill was able to somehow send a message and get us off the island.

Bill said quietly, "I'm sorry, Ray, I can't find a way to send a message. I've tried looking in different rooms, but there's nothing to signal with to the agency. So whatever it is going to take, we have to make it out of here alive! Also, there are rooms that we are restricted to on the other side of the mansion; there are armed guards there, and one almost caught me snooping around. Maybe that's where they keep these creatures or something. I've noticed a lot of cameras inside the mansion and outside hidden in trees and other areas, like we are always being watched."

Bill hands me a small piece of paper. "Go to your room and memorize this paper, then rip it up in very tiny pieces and flush it down the toilet. If something happens to me and you can get off this island, go to this place I wrote for you on the paper and tell them everything that has happened here."

I left to go to my room to do as Bill asked. There are only two tables left, and only two players are exempt from going out tonight. Bill and I are at the same table again—what terrible luck. On top of it, it's a bad night of card playing for me, and then Bill and I are out both and will be partners again in the night. I wonder how long our luck is going to last.

After two more hours of waiting, the game finally ends, and the two winners are loud and joyous as they left the room. We walk over to the table where all the losers have gathered, and we get ready to view the creature that is to come for us tonight. There are three cards on the table. A card is turned over by the last player that went out. The hostess holds the card up: it's a picture of a tall, thin, burned-skinned creature wearing tattered dark clothing. He has glowing yellow eyes and ears that seem small, like they have been burnt off. He is wearing a black beanie hat and has long, thick knives somehow attached to his burned hands and arms.

I start thinking, "This is the last night! We just need to get through this night."

The hostess says, "Everyone head over to the weapons room and get your weapons." Bill and I pick our usual crossbows. All the players gather at the exit door, and I look around at the few players left. There have been eight players killed so far. Horrifying!

The hostess states, "Players, please leave the mansion." Everyone gathers in their usual groups and start to head out quietly into the jungle, each group disappearing into the night. Bill and I stay behind and let the others go for their spots.

As we get to our spot and settle in, we can hear a group down below us, not that far away. Bill and I look at each other, and I say, "This isn't good. Hopefully they don't attract the creature our way."

We wait. It's been a long and quiet night, and we don't say much. Bill says, "I think we're good for the night. The birds are starting to do their morning chirping, and the sun should come up in a short while." We don't hear any screams in the night and think maybe it's a good night for everyone. Not long after Bill says that, we start to hear screams and they're coming from close by, down below us!

We freeze. I'm having a hard time breathing, and my heart is racing. I don't want to move and make any noise. I listen and can hear the group trying to fight the creature. It sounds horrible, and they sound like they are not doing so good. We listen to the screams of a couple guys, who seem to be in horrific pain. We lie down and face toward the trail going down to where the group is, and we get ready to fire our weapons if we need to.

We hear someone or something coming fast our way. It's so dark that we see only a slight silhouette, and we aren't taking any chances. We open fire with the cross bows, afraid that the creature has our scent and is coming for us. We aim and fire our bows as fast as we can. The crossbow holds five arrows apiece, and we empty them in seconds. We finish firing and hurry down our escape trail, hoping that we stopped or killed whatever was coming at us.

We meet at our designated rally spot and quickly reload and wait, but nobody comes. The sun rises, and we are able live for one more day! Now it will be up to one of us to beat The Man and win this card tournament.

Bill and I head back for the mansion, walking fast. Both of us are more confident and have somewhat renewed hope.

Bill asks me what I would do with the money, and I say, "Well, when I have it, then I will be ready to give the answer! Bill, I hope it's me or you that wins this, and that we both end up safely getting out of here and having a good life after all this, whether it's with or without the prize money."

Bill says, "Thanks buddy. I hope tomorrow we're both sitting safely on a beach in the Cayman Islands, far away from this hell hole!" We enter the mansion, turn in our weapons, and say our good-byes before going to our rooms. I quickly shower, pour a full glass of whiskey, and sit on my bed. I think, "I really need to relax and get focused on something other than this tournament." I debate on whether to relax and get some much-needed sleep, but instead I go to the ballroom.

I make my way down to the ballroom, and my eyes focus on a tall blonde European, and as I approached her she says, "Hej," which means hello in Swedish. "My name is Monic, and it's very nice to meet you." I stare at her for a second. She is very beautiful and wears a tight-fitting, seventies style go-go dress with high black boots. Her hair is long and pulled tightly back.

We speak some more and enjoy a few stiff drinks, and it really takes my mind off being in this horrific place. We head to my room and have a great time with each other. After she leaves, I begin to feel relaxed again, thinking, "Now that I have a clearer head, I will be ready to play this so-called Man."

CHAPTER 10

DAY FIVE—THE FINAL DAY

RAY: I leave the room saying to myself, "The final day has finally come." I walk slowly down to the lunchroom and make a couple of sandwiches. There are only five players me, Bill, this young guy named Dave, and the two guys who had won their tables the night before. I ask Dave, "Where are the rest of the guys?"

Dave says with a quiet voice, "We're it! There were four people killed by that creature last night. The group was unable to fight the creature off as it came after us." Dave is a young professional poker player who is lucky to have lived this long. Bill and I listen to Dave as he tells his story about what happened last night.

"We staged our small group around a large tree in the jungle's darkness, and we thought we were going to make it through the night because the sun was coming up soon. Then out of nowhere, we saw the creature. It was walking quickly in a searching pattern, leaving no space untouched. It went left for a while then turned right, and then headed left again. It was only a matter of time before it got to us.

"The creature started to get closer and closer, and then it looked over and spotted us. With no hesitation it ran directly at us, set to kill us. It started viciously attacking our group, showing no mercy! Guys started crying out as they were getting cut to pieces. My partner and I panicked, and we ran up a steep, small trail that was behind us. "We ran for only a couple minutes. Then some things came flying in the air at us. Whatever they were, they took down my friend. I was trying to duck out of the way of it, but my foot hit a rock, and I fell and rolled out of control down the side of a cliff. I don't know what happened to my partner, but I never saw him again.

Bill and I look at each other, thinking that explains who was running our way. We don't say to Dave that we were in the same area as the group, and that we fired our weapons at someone or something. It wouldn't have changed anything anyways to say something, so we didn't.

I let Bill continue to talk with Dave while I poured a whiskey on the rocks and started to think, "It's time to get my head together. It's the time for the final table, and time to get ready to beat The Man and get the hell off this fucking island alive, and hopefully with the money!"

As we walk together and enter the poker room, we see The Man is sitting and waiting alone at the final table for us. He seems to be in his late sixties and is dressed in a black tuxedo. He has long white hair that is combed back. He is a very distinguished and professional looking man, but he has an evil presence about him.

The hostess speaks up from behind the poker table. "Welcome, gentlemen to the final table. Please take your seats."

Ray: As we walk up to our table and look at our assigned seats, I see I'm going to be sitting next to Bill, Dave is on the right side of Bill, and the two other guys are sitting to the far left. The Man is sitting by himself in the far right seat.

I am feeling somewhat comfortable; I have been in many large and televised tournaments and have also won a few of them. When a player sits down at that final table, he has to have complete control of emotions and endure the pressures that are placed on him in order to be the best he can, or else the other players will sense his weakness and take him out. It is the job of each individual player to make sure he is emotionally sound and ready to play; he is relying only on himself, and there are no coaches or time outs—it's just him and the other players.

Normally, if we lose, then we're finished and go home, and we're not winning the big money, but in this case, we could lose our lives!

Dave: Taking my assigned seat and sitting at the final table. My heart is racing, sweat is dripping down my forehead, and I'm feeling clammy. I look around at all the players at the table; they're professionals and are showing that their calm, ready to play. I know they are all nervous inside, but that's why it's called a poker face: they're able to hide their emotions no matter the situation.

There is a lot at stake at this final table: money, freedom, and life. I'm feeling okay; I've been in this position before. The stakes are high, and I have done well at times like this. Pressure is what you make of it; it can be overcome and used to your advantage. But playing for my life and my freedom is definitely another story.

I try to get my head clear, but I keep thinking back at what has transpired here these past five days. It is definitely luck that I've made it this far, that's for sure." I was with the same group of guys for each night we went out, and unfortunately we had someone from our group killed in each night. On this last night, I don't really know what happened, but I was the only one to make it out alive! I became somewhat friends with all those players, and tonight the worst feeling I have is that they are all dead now.

We talked about how we had entered this tournament, and all of us were approached by the same man dressed in black. It sounded like one of those ultimate tournaments that we hear about, that comes around once in a lifetime. The best players in the world are put together for one special and private tournament, and the players need no entry fee, because the person hosting the event allows only people to place bets on who will win the tournament. The betters are treated to high luxury and have to pay a minimum entry fee. That money takes care of the players' winnings, the winning better or betters, and the person hosting the unique event. Maybe this is how this tournament is played, but nothing was told to us, and we cannot see any of the betters.

The whole time on this island, I kept somewhat to myself, not making any close friends, only acquaintances. It was very difficult for me to accept that every day as we played, someone I played next to or joked with at the poker table might be killed later that night.

Every night that I went out into that jungle, I chose a sword that looked like it came from Japan's samurai era. It was made out of some of the finest detail and workmanship I have ever seen. My uncle has an old sword collection, that I have trained with and I've seen many old, traditional swords in different dojos, but I have never seen a sword of that caliber. The owner of this weapons collection has a very respectable weapons room and a very diverse knowledge of weaponry. With all the weapons to choose from in the weapons room, the player is in a very difficult position, having to think and use good judgment to choose a suitable weapon, as well as being able to handle the weapon and use it to successfully to defend himself.

Thinking back on my last night, as our group was sitting around the tree, quietly waiting, I was beginning to think we were going to get lucky, but luck has a funny way of ending quickly. Then it happened. Walking back and forth searching the areas like a dog looks for its lost bone; the creature came and went, in and out of the moonlight. It was very scary, and we could see the large swords he was carrying. He would disappear in the shadows and then reappear.

Everyone saw him and looked on it with terror in their hearts. It was eventually going to reach us, and we hoped the sun would come up and we would all be safe! One other guy that was sitting next to me was named George. I leaned over to him and said quietly, "If it comes and we can't defend against it, let's run up this steep cliff behind us." George agreed and gave a nod.

The sun did not make it in time, and the creature with its glowing yellow eyes and large knives came fast upon us, striking the players that were in front of him and severing arms. Players' faces were mangled and sliced wide open. It was a bloody brutal attack.

As our group fought the horrific creature, the screams of my fellow players started to die out as they were slashed to death. George and I were overwhelmed by the loud terrified screams, and we made a break and ran up the steep mountain behind us. George was running in front of me, and it was very dark. We ran for at least a few minutes, and I was getting out of breath. I could only hear the noise George made running up the mountain in front of me.

All of a sudden George let out a scream, and then I started hearing things flying all around me. They sounded like bats or something. I tripped over a rock and fell down a steep decline, rolling out of control. I didn't break anything, but my whole body was in pain. I laid there in a fetal position, out of breath. I remained still and quiet till the sun came up only a short time later.

When the sun came up, I was so relieved. I looked at my scrapes and open cuts, and they were nothing major. I headed up the steep incline where I had rolled down and looked for George, but there was no sign of him. "He must have already made it to the mansion," I thought.

I saw the entrance to the mansion in the distance and started to run toward it. I wanted to get to it as fast as I could and get out of this horrific jungle, never to return back to it! As I ran to the mansion, I thought, 'If I get off this island alive, my head will never be the same." I turned in my weapon and tried to relax in my room. I looked at myself in the mirror; I was white as a ghost. I grabbed a tequila bottle and had four quick shots, and then I took a hot shower for at least fifteen minutes till I felt very drained. With one more tequila shot, I passed out as soon as my head hit the pillow.

When I woke, my heart was still beating a million miles an hour. It was time to get ready for the final game, and I was feeling somewhat ready, whatever the outcome was going to be. I was ready to get this all over with!

CHAPTER 11

FINAL GAME

"Welcome players! Today is the final table, and I want to congratulate you on making it this far. If someone is able to beat The Man and win the final table, the money will be wired to an account in a bank located in the Cayman Islands. Also, here is a plane ticket for a flight that will leave tonight, also to the Cayman Islands."

The plane ticket was sitting on the table and was shown to us.

The Man stood up and spoke. He was a big but fit man, around 230 pounds and six foot four. He looked around with his dark, piercing eyes at each of us players. With a deep, harsh voice he says, "Whoever loses today will have a chance to get off my island. Five boats are at the dock, one for each of you. The boats are located on the far side of my island. The boats are all programmed to take you to a private dock, far away from here. On your way to the boat dock, you will have to survive my six beautiful creatures, which will be out hunting for you as you try to make it to your boat. If and when you make it to the boats, you have nothing more to worry about and will be safe.

"One more thing. This tournament has never happened, and you will tell no one of this place or what has taken place here—or else I will have the enjoyment of taking my creatures to hunt down you and your families." A sickened smile appears on his face. "Good luck and congratulations on making it this far, let the final game begin!"

The cards are dealt, and the game has officially started. I start out with some high cards, and everything is feeling and going good; I win the first two hands. Bill has gotten good cards also, and he is looking and feeling confident and wins a couple hands as well. The young kid Dave must want to get this final game done with, because his mind is definitely not in the game. He is nervous and is talking fast. The two guys who won their tables the night before came with the strategy to call every all-in.

As the two players try to take someone out early, each one is playing for the quick win, trying to take The Man out by betting high. But the strategy is backfiring as The Man has good cards also, and is calling them. As the first player goes all-in, The Man calls and takes him out of the game, and the player is quickly escorted to the weapons room. The very next hand, a second player bets all-in, and just like the guy before him, The Man calls and takes him out.

Bill and I just look at each other, shaking our heads. Now The Man has tripled his chips and is going to be that much harder to take out. The Man stares at Dave and asks him, "Your father is a professional poker player, right?" Dave says, "Yes, he is—he's the best!" The Man replies, "The best?" He lets out a small laugh. "He is good. I wanted to find out for myself. I tried to get him to come to the last tournament I had, but he declined. So I'm happy you had the balls to come, unlike your father. We will see if he taught you well." The Man gives another sick smile.

On the next hand, right after the flop, Dave quickly says, "All-in," and The Man calls with a big grin on his face, saying, "Well, we shall see how good you are, Dave!" Bill and I fold and look on; this could be good for Dave. At least, I hope it is. Dave turns over his cards with a little smile: he has a jack and a queen, with a jack, queen, and a nine on the table. He is in very good shape with a two pair.

The Man keeps his cards down, not showing them. The next card turned over is the three of hearts, and the final card is the two of diamonds. The Man looks at Dave, who has a smile on his face, and says, "Nice try, Dave. "He lays down a pair of nines, and with a nine on the table, he has three of a kind. Now I see why he's called The Man. Dave sits there for a moment, speechless. He now has to go back through the jungle. He gets up and leaves the table quietly, shaking hands and saying good-bye to Bill and then me. He doesn't say anything to The Man. He is escorted to the weapons room and is let out the back door.

The dealer says, "Are you ready, gentlemen? Cards are dealt, and we get back to the game. It is back and forth: I win a hand, then Bill, then The Man. It goes on for hours.

Bill catches a real good hand and slow plays it, and The Man falls for it, putting almost all of his chips in the pot. The Man has a hardened grin on his face and lays down two pair, sixes and jacks. Bill looks at The Man with a smile and says, "Maybe next time." He lays down two pair, jacks and nines. Bill takes the large pot in and stacks his large pile of chips, looking over at me and giving a wink and a little smile.

After a couple hands of me winning, we have The Man down to only a few chips, and we can tell he is very agitated. The next hand the blinds go up, and The Man has the big blind, putting him in with almost all of his chips. I figure it is time, and I ask, "Can we make some sort of a deal?" I say it with a partial smile on my face. I can see The Man get agitated as he looks at me with those blackened eyes. "When Bill or I beat you, can we split the money and go free out the front door?"

The Man seemingly has no sense of humor, giving a motionless glare at me and then at Bill. He clenches his fists on top of the table and says loudly, "There is only one plane ticket and one winner!"

I take the hint. It was worth a try, and I am happy to see that he is getting even more agitated. The Man goes all-in with what chips he has left, and Bill has good cards and calls as I fold. Bill has a pair of kings and is able to take out The Man, who has a pair of tens. I feel proud of Bill and can see huge relief in his face and body. The Man wastes no time in saying loudly, "There are still two players left; the one with all the chips is the winner."

I comment, "Since you're out, isn't there a weapon in the weapons room with your name on it? Or an escort waiting to take you out of the mansion?" The Man stares at me in disbelief, and then he lets me have it. He lets out some pent-up anger. "The weapons room has plenty of knives that will take a tongue off, and if you say one more thing like that, I would be happy to oblige!"

I am happy I got to him, but I keep a straight face, which pisses off The Man even more. Soon Bill and I come to the quick realization that one of us will live and go free and be very rich and one of us might be left here to die a horrible death! We did however come for the money, and it's good to be playing against a friend, so we play on.

The next hand Bill says with a grin, "All-in," without looking at his cards. "Ray, do the same. Let's let it ride on one hand. Let's let fate help decide the new millionaire." I say, "Okay, Bill, let's do it." I'm thinking to myself, "This will be the most important hand I will ever be dealt."

The cards are dealt, and The Man stands up and looks at our cards on the table. My adrenalin starts to go up as I look at my hand and feel my heart race. I want to smile but keep a straight face. I have a pair of aces and think, "For sure I will win." Bill has the ten and nine of spades, and he sits back in his chair and looks up as if to ask for help from above.

The dealer puts a smile on her face and then says, "Ready, gentlemen?" She flips the first three cards over for the flop. The cards are the four and eight of spades, and one card that will do neither of us any good, a three of hearts. I immediately think, "This can't be happening. Spades! What are the chances? Can Bill pull off a flush?"

We all look on to see what the next card is. It's the four of hearts, no help for Bill or me. I feel my face start to flush, and my body is hot. I'm on the verge of passing out! I grab my drink and quickly finish my whiskey. I feel a little better and ask the hostess, "Please bring me one more, quickly!"

I look up toward the ceiling as Bill did earlier and say a quick prayer, praying that a spade does not come up. The final card is laid face down on the table. Once turned over, it will instantly change my or Bill's life forever. The card will be the cause for one of us to go and face death and for the other to go free and have great wealth.

The room is silent, the focus being on the card that lays there on the table. The dealer reaches and flips the card over. We all stand up and lean over the table to look. It's the jack of spades. Bill had the flush! Bill lets out a sigh of relief, and then he looks up and says, "Thank you, Lord."

I almost pass out. My body is at its breaking point; this tournament has taken everything out of me. I slowly catch my breath and recover, sitting back down in my chair and thinking, "What a card game." At least it was my new friend that won. If it was back in Vegas, I would be very happy with second. It would have been a huge payday, and tonight would be one hell of a party. I sit there speechless, and then with what energy I can pull together, I say, "Congratulations." Bill reaches over and shakes my hand tightly. I could feel his sweaty palm, and I tell him, "Best of luck with your new life."

The Man is sitting across from me, and he looks mad that he didn't win. Maybe these tournaments have gone on in the past, and maybe no one has ever beaten him until today. The Man acts professional and reaches over to congratulate Bill. He gives him the plane ticket and shows him the completion of the money wire transfer on the computer.

Then The Man reaches over and grabs Bill hard by the arm, bringing Bill in close to him. I can hear what he says in his distinct, stern voice. "There will always be someone watching you, Bill." Then he looks over at me with those black piercing eyes and says, "If you are able to stay alive and make it off my island,

"He gives me a half smile and looks back over at Bill. "You guys will never speak of this game to anyone. To no one! Do you understand me?" He says in a stronger, louder, mean voice, "Otherwise there will be serious consequences for you and for any of your loved ones. You can take my word on that." I am still in shock as I sit there and look around the room. What is truly terrifying is that just five day ago, so many players came here, and unfortunately they are never going to return to their homes or loved ones.

Bill slaps me on the arm and says, "Snap out of it." I stand up and shake hands with him, and then he brings me in close and gives me a hard hug. He whispers in my ear, "Wait as long as you can in our spot. Once I leave here, I'm killing whoever is there with me, and I'm making the call. Wait for me; I will come back for you."

I said loudly, "Good-bye, Bill" and then give a nod to The Man, and I am escorted to the familiar weapons room. The weapons door is opened, and I pick the weapon of choice for Bill and me. Before I am escorted out the back door I look back one last time, and Bill is standing by the card table looking at me.

Bill yells out, "The Cayman Islands, that's where we will go. Good luck, Ray, and stay alive!" I give a quick wave to Bill and walk out the door. As I walk away from the mansion, I think, "How long can I stay alive? I need to try and stay alive long enough to be saved by Bill's agency guys." I have some hope, though. "When I make it off this hellish island, I'm going to look forward to the Cayman Islands!

BILL

Watching my friend walk out the door I feel very worried for him. Ray was my new brother and I do not want to see anything happen to him. I resolve that I will do everything in my power to keep him alive. Looking back at the man and his evil demeanor and eyes, "congratulations Bill you have done very well, I will say this you are the first to have ever beat me."

I will escort you to the front door and from there my security staff will personally escort you off the island "and remember our deal Bill, I will always be watching." "I will sir' I say back so as not to alarm him that I know his scheme to have me killed, and that he is saying this to keep my guard down. I reach the front door as the man holds out his clammy hand and a quick shake it was good bye. Three well-built men dressed in black suits are waiting at the door. One speaks up and says "congratulations Bill, we will be your escorts, you are home free."

We walk down to a large upscale speedboat that is tied to the pier.

On the way to the island

Five military Blackhawk choppers are headed toward the island, Bill yells out to the pilot "it is getting dark, we do not have much time, and we have to find him. He is on the high ground close to the mansion." Coming closer to the island the large mansion is now in plain sight, and the high ground can be seen.

"There! There is where Ray is waiting." Getting closer a group of those hideous creatures can be seen headed up toward Rays position.

Bill yells out "fire at those fucking monsters," and the 50 cal opens up lighting up the mountain, one pass then another till there is no movement. "There he is," as they can see Ray huddled around a tree. "Put the halo down in that open area."

They hear a huge explosion as the mansion goes up in flames, Bills priority is to get Ray, and eight men and Bill secure the area as Ray comes running down and meets Bill and gives him a hard hug. Ray has tears in his eyes "I don't believe it, I was a goner if you didn't show up when you did." More shots are fired by the automatic weapons as they make sure each of the creatures are fully dead.

Ray says" how did you do it, how did you get everyone here?" "After the man left me at the door with three of his men to take me to the boat, I knew they were going to kill me, so taking them by surprise and killing them, then I took the boat to the first house I saw and I used their phone to notify the agency."

Ray said "I'm really glad to see you brother, I owe you my life." We hear over the radio "The man has not been captured—the evidence in the mansion is all destroyed.

Part II:
Anna's Empowered Legacy

Eight Years Later

CHAPTER 1

THE START OF A NEW BEGINNING

Bill

I awake in the blackness of night. It's very hot, with only the smell of rotting carnage and smoke in the air. I lie silent, still staring up into the darkness and not fully awake, wondering if anyone is out there. I am in bed with my hand on my rifle, silent and not breathing, just listening as I wait for that sound that will make me get up and either welcome my fellow countrymen or, if it's my enemy, I will have to kill them!

I hold my breath, listening for any noise. There is no one to confirm if they've heard anything. I start to nod off when a cold breeze enters the room. I keep still and open my eyes, wondering if this is my imagination. But I feel the cold air again as it passes by my bed and then seems to come back and surround my bed.

I realize there is something in the room! I'm now fully awake and try to get up, but as I try to move there is a cold force that holds my body tight, like nothing I've ever felt before. I feel like I'm paralyzed. Then as soon as it started, it ends and the cold leaves.

My blood is pumping! Now able to sit up, I turn the flashlight on and use it to look around the room, but there is nothing here. My heart is beating hard, and I say, "This must have been a bad dream, what a crazy dream!" I stay up for a little while and calm back down. I'm able to fall back to sleep. When I awake again, It's morning, I can tell from the light that passes through some of the bullet holes in the wall. It's time to get up and make the rounds. I'm feeling tired and still wondering what happened last night.

Getting dressed and grabbing my AK-47 I begin my daily area search. As I walk the warehouse areas, I see and hear no one, only a couple of crows that are hanging around making some noise. I walk by a stack of smelly, rotting bodies that my team killed four days ago. During the fight no one else made it out alive, neither my guys nor the enemies. It was some of the fiercest and deadliest fights I have ever been involved in.

As I look at the enemies' dead bodies, which are stacked in a pile, one soldier stands out. He has a look to him, his face is very strange. He's a very pale, white color with large black eyes that are still open.

He lies there with an expression on his face, as if he's looking at me. I remember this soldier, he was their leader, a very fierce fighter. He moved very fast and yelled out orders to his men. But he wasn't fast enough for my sniper rifle, and he took a direct hit and with it a huge hole in his chest.

When I killed their leader, they were really pissed off, and it was fierce fighting from then on. We lost guys as fast as they were losing guys, and shots and screams rang out in the thick smoke. I was shooting one bullet after another from my sniper position on the second-floor tower, and after a few large explosions and a lot of firing, the smoke started to clear and everything went silent. There was no one moving, no more shooting, and I couldn't get anyone on the radio. I realized I was alone!

We were a forward element of eight special-ops guys, and we took our position in this large, abandoned warehouse, out in the distance. It was desert terrain, with no other buildings for miles. We could see our forces and the enemies in the very brutal fighting, and with the loss of contact from our main unit, I could tell things were not going good for our side.

As I went to sleep that night, I left my flashlight on to make sure if I had to get up in the night, I would be able to see. I slept very lightly that night, lying there with the anticipation of that cold, paralyzing feeling coming back again. I awoke suddenly and grabbed for my weapon, thinking I heard something.

I look around the room, and all is well. I lay there for another minute, silent, trying to hear anything, but there is nothing.

The warehouse is booby-trapped in case anyone was to try to get in and up toward my room. I used booby traps that the enemy is unfamiliar with. If my side sees a booby trap like the ones I made, they will know instantly that there are friendly forces in the area.

As I lay back down, I start to fall asleep. That's when the flashlight starts to go on and off, and I think and hope it's just the batteries. I say, "I just put new batteries in," I turn the flashlight off and then back on, shaking it a little. It stays back on, and I fall back asleep . . . but I awake to darkness and to that cold feeling again.

I lay there with my eyes open, afraid to move. I can sense something is out there in the darkness, and I try to reach for my flashlight but am unable to move. I am paralyzed.

As I lay there helpless, I begin to fall asleep and dream of faces of men that I have killed before. Then out of the darkness I see the face of that leader I killed a few days ago. His face, his black eyes are staring directly at me; it is just him and me in a large, dimly lit tent. He is sitting across from me, only a few feet away, and he begins to laugh in an evil tone. I look around because there is more light now, and now there are more chairs, four on each side of me, with men tied up to them and their hands bound behind the chair.

Their chairs are up against the tent wall. The man in the dream, the enemy leader, yells out firm orders, but I can't hear anything he says; I only see his lips and his crazed facial expressions. Then he stands up and reaches against the wall, holding up a baseball bat. He starts to pace back and forth, yelling out something. I am also in a chair, strapped in and unable to move. Then I slowly begin to hear his voice become clearer: he is instructing everyone to put their heads against the tent wall. Everyone does so, and he says loudly, "Do not move!"

I will call him Delta, for devil, because I have never seen a man so un alive before. He leaves the tent, and I look down to the right side of me down to the first man in the chair. His head is against the back of the tent, and he isn't moving, looking straight ahead. All of a sudden I can see the back of his head explode, and his body falls forward, lifeless. Delta is using the baseball bat on each head indentation on the tent wall. The next guy and then the next guy, all their heads are smashed in. The guy next to me is screaming; he is paralyzed from moving away, and he's next! His screams are so loud, and as I listen, I begin to recognize the soldier's voice. I look over at him and realize he was my friend and teammate who died during the fight in the warehouse.

I become hysterical—these are not ordinary men, these are my men! The screaming stops, and I am covered in his blood as the back of his head explodes all over the floor and me. I cannot move, I am now in a paralyzed state and feel a power from behind me, forcing my head against the side of the tent. I wait to have my head bashed in. I can't believe this is happening, and I scream out in anger.

I am waiting for my turn . . . but it doesn't come, and now I'm able to move my head. I look over at my former teammate to my left, the next victim after me. His body is bent forward and motionless, and I realize his brains and blood are also all over me. Delta skipped me and went down the other side. Suddenly I wake up. It's daylight, and I'm lying in a pool of sweat, my heart screaming. I am so angry at the memory of Delta's face, and that horrific dream with me and my men.

Quickly getting dressed and making my way down to see the enemy bodies; all are in the same position. I say to myself, "I'm going to burn these evil bodies." I find a gas can lying around and pour it on their corpses, lighting the match and wasting no time. I say to them, "Burn in hell" and watch them as they go up in flames. A fierce, cold breeze goes right through me, almost knocking me down. I say, "I know that was you, you evil piece of shit," as I look at Delta's face, who still seems like he is staring at me.

The room fills with smoke and the awful smell of burnt bodies and carnage. I began to think all this smoke is going to attract attention to my location. The enemy or my guys will see the smoke, but I don't care, there is no way I can stay here in this hell hole much longer. Four hours pass, and as I thought, someone has seen the flames because there is a convoy coming. I grab my sniper rifle and go on the second-story balcony to take a look. To my relief it's my military. I wait in front of the warehouse for my guys to arrive. We do a short debrief, I quickly gather a few of my things, and we immediately start back to a base fifty miles west of here.

The striker vehicle is dark, hot, and very noisy, but I don't care. I'm very exhausted and happy to have left that warehouse. I'm in good hands now with my fellow troops, and I begin to fall asleep, exhausted. I fall into a deep sleep, only to dream of Delta's face again, with those black eyes staring at me, piercing through me. I begin to have a flashback, one by one, of the horrific sights and screams of my team, their heads bashed in by Delta and that fucking baseball bat.

I awake suddenly to screaming and darkness. I feel my face, and it has hot blood and tissue all over it, I immediately think that we are in a firefight! An explosion of some sort must have taken out the striker. I try to move but am barely able to. It's very dark and smoky, and I can barely breathe. It feels like I am breathing in fire. I feel the hot blood from my fellow soldiers start to harden on my face, and the wet blood and thick smoke in my eyes prevents me from seeing anything.

Unable to move and or see to get out, I feel terrible pain all over my body. Then out of nowhere, I feel a cold sensation around me, as if something is here with me. A voice seems to come out of the darkness: "Move, move!" I hear it over and over again, and a cold feeling is all around me, giving me the energy to move and the direction to go.

I begin to crawl. The smoke is very bad, and the heat is unbearable. I feel I cannot make it! But I feel the cold sensation get stronger all around; it's staying with me, and I find the strength to keep going. I keep crawling and don't' stop. I still cannot see, but then as I crawl a few feet more, I can see some light. As I crawl harder and I see more light, out of nowhere I am grabbed hard, and I feel I am being dragged.

I feel unbearable pain all over my body, and I can see now, I am being bandaged up by two soldiers. One looks at me with a half smile and tells me, "I didn't think you would make it, but you will be okay. We stopped the bleeding and patched you up." My vision is getting clearer, and I look around. Everything is burning, it smells horrible, and it's hot and very hard to breathe.

Out of nowhere there is another explosion. I feel the blast, and a bad concussion feeling comes over me as the air is sucked right out of my lungs, I am in a black fog again. I feel I cannot move, hearing nothing and seeing nothing, just lying there paralyzed and trying to catch my breath and get my bearing.

There's a horrible ringing in my ears that won't stop. I lay there unable to move, and after a minute I start to get my senses back. The ringing finally goes, and I try to move and fully catch my breath. I feel something heavy is on top of me, and I push a little. Now I'm able to see some sunlight. I push harder and move the body off of me, and I try to sit up just enough to see the situation going on around me, the enemy might be out there. I look around but see nothing is moving. There is a lot of thick smoke, and as the wind moves it around, I see more and more of the destruction. I look at the bloody and mangled body that is lying next to me: it's the medic who was just patching me up. I feel for his pulse but there is none. I look around for the other soldier who was working on me, but I don't see him; maybe he got thrown from the blast.

I lay there and look around for another minute. There is no movement, only thick smoke everywhere, burning vehicles, and what seems to be no life! I get up and grab an AK that's lying on the ground and go around to check the area and the bodies. As I'm checking, I see everyone is badly blown to pieces. It's a saddening and horrific sight, to see my fellow countrymen like this.

There must be more than twenty dead. "Someone had to have made it,' but as I check the last few bodies, I realize I'm alone again!

I don't see any enemies, so it must had been a large IED that we hit, and then someone must have accidentally set off a second set of explosions; it was probably a daisy chain of explosives that that killed everything in our area.

I look around, and there is nothing serviceable. I can see in the distance the warehouse; I know there is some safety there, and it has supplies I need. I feel sick and almost pass out from exhaustion as I start to walk to the warehouse. I awake in darkness, but there is a little light from the moon, coming through holes in the wall. I lie still and gather my senses. I am in a bed, and I recognize the bullet holes in the wall I'm in the room where I slept before, back in the warehouse! I regain my composure and try to remember how I got here.

I don't remember anything, so I must have blacked out. I do remember the bad explosion, and I remember everyone is dead, but that's it. "Maybe it was all a bad dream?" I try to move but am in horrible pain. I feel very weak and pass out again.

I awaken to light coming from the bullet holes in the wall, as I've done the many times before.

I try to move but feel pain all over my body, and I say to myself, "I have to look at my wounds." They look like they're all bad, because there is a lot of dried blood. I'm back in this unholy place. I don't want to be back here!" I realize that for now that I have no choice and will have to stay.

I don't remember getting here; I must have a bad concussion. I try to get up but feel myself getting lightheaded. My body is still in a tremendous amount of pain, I have a bad headache, and I feel my strength going down to nothing.

I awake in a pool of sweat and say to myself, "I must get up, or I'll die here." I start to get up, and it's very painful, but I get up out of bed. All those years of hard fighting in the military taught me to never give up and do what needs to get done, no matter how much pain and discomfort I'm in.

I have some water and some MRE food lying around, and it's enough to make me feel a little better. I take a quick look at my bandages: from what the medics were able to do, they did a good job; all the bandages are still tight. I will clean them later after I know it's safe outside. I search the perimeter and make sure I'm not alone

CHAPTER 2

THE NEW GUESTS

I grab a weapon that's lying on the floor that was a rifle with a scope and walk downstairs. I gave my teammates an honorable burial, but as I walk to the next room by the burned carnage of the enemy bodies, I am horrified to see that Delta has not burned! Only burned-up bodies and ashes lay on top of his body. This time I notice there is a different grin on his face, one of anger, and those eyes are piercing seemingly right through me. I try to look away but stay focused on them.

I begin to have flashbacks of Delta's face, sitting in that chair in the tent staring at me. Then I flash back to me riding in the striker vehicle. I try to look away, but I remain focused on the Delta. A cold breeze comes out of nowhere and seems to go right through me, sending me to my knees.

I'm free from looking at the Delta, and turn away. I get up and hurry to leave that area and go up to another spot, where the lookout tower is. I look out in the distance, and nothing is out there; it's safe for now, but for how much longer? The enemy has to see the smoke and will probably come back to collect souvenirs and make sure everyone is dead.

I can't leave this place yet, I have no choice but to stay here and rest and try to heal, plus I don't have a vehicle to leave with, and the desert heat will surely finish me off in no time if I try to walk out of here, especially in my condition.

I go to a part of the warehouse where I have some medical supplies stored and tend to my wounds. I have a bad cut to my upper leg, and I slowly take the bandage off; I don't want to reopen my wound, so I'm extra careful with the bandage. Once that's done I gently wash it with soap and bottled water, put some iodine on it, and re-bandage it with a fresh dressing. I do the same for my side and arm and head.

I'm feeling better now that I've seen my wounds; they're bad and could use some stitches, but I can manage them for now. I feel very exhausted, so I go back up to my room, setting up booby traps as I go. I sit on my bed and eat some MREs and say to myself, "I have to try to get some sleep." My head is pounding, my body is in pain, and I'm feeling very weak. Still, I say to myself, "I'm very lucky to be alive." I take a couple pain pills and lie down and feel myself pass right out.

I wake up to the sunlight coming through the holes in the wall. I must have slept through the whole night, no Delta dreams, and I am feeling a little better. I get up and look at my wounds, making sure none reopened in the night. Then I grab my weapon and start to make my rounds, defusing my traps as I go. I don't go by Delta's area this time and head right for the second floor landing to watch out in the distance for the enemy. The only thing to look at is a little smoke coming from some of the burned out vehicles.

I look through the scope for any signs of life, and there is none. There are only a few desert rodents running around, and a lot of burned scrap metal from all the hard fighting out there.

I think back, remembering my men. I would like to see them again. I really miss them, they were a great bunch of guys. I would do anything for them. We were a tight group, and some of us knowing each other for years, and we spent a lot of time with each other and our families, having barbeques and kids' parties; we were all a tight family!

I had a beautiful wife and two sons, ages four and six, and I miss them the most. Many of my fellow team members' families died when the city was attacked, and we all stuck together to take an oath of revenge. We joined the resistance as a small special-ops team. I was the leader, and we put our wives and kids into hiding. Once we started fighting, it was terrible and brutal, and there was no leaving the front lines to go back to our families.

After three months of fierce fighting we were told that the town our families were hiding in had been overrun, and everyone in the town was killed. It was a horrible day for me and my teammates.

I think of all the things I've been through in the military special forces, then all I went through with the CIA and shutting down that horrible poker tournament with the island of creatures and The Man and when his men found me and my buddy Ray hiding out in the Cayman Islands, and they had their killing squad come in the night and they killed Ray and almost killed me. I was back on the run and had to go deep into hiding and make a new life for myself, where I thought that I would be safe and would just settle down, and everything would be okay.

Getting the news of losing my family was the worst news that I have ever received. I could deal with whatever happened to me, but mine or any of my team's families, that was the worst. Now all this stuff is happening in an evil warehouse, and it's very difficult to keep a sane mind!

As I am looking out into the far distance, I can see what looks like a cloud of dust. I think it's a vehicle and grab my sniper rifle to look through the scope. It's actually three vehicles. As I sight in, it seems like two vehicles are chasing the front one, and there are men hanging out of the windows of the two vehicles shooting at the first. The first vehicle seems like its headed straight for me, and as they start to get closer, I can get a clearer view of them. The lead vehicle is a large SUV of some sort, but the two following are definitely armored Humvees—the kind and color that my enemy drives!

The driver of the SUV seems to be evading the other two pretty well. I sight in through the scope and can see three people in the first Humvee and three in the second. I wait for them to get in range and sight in at the second Humvee's driver's chest, and with a slow and steady squeeze like I've done many times before, I pull the trigger. The Humvee goes out of control for a second and then slows to a stop.

I sight in for the driver of the first Humvee, and with a deep breath and a slow exhale, staying nice and calm, I pull the trigger. "Nice shot!" I say to myself as the vehicle also slow and then stops. It is a headshot to the driver. The two shooters get out and continue to fire at the SUV.

I begin to take aim at the shooters and snipe off each one. I have a lot of frustration built up for this enemy, so I'm going to make each one pay. I fire at one of the shooters and make a nice headshot. I take aim and shoot at the leg of the shooter who is firing from behind a door; the bullet takes part of his leg off, and he immediately falls to the ground. I know he is I terrible pain, and I smile.

I sight in at the next target and fire. The shot takes off a section of his arm at the shoulder like it was butter, and he goes down with blood spewing all over. Now it's time to sight in on the last shooter. I look around and I find him, take aim for his lower body, and fire. It's a gut shot and almost cuts him in half. I watch for a second as he lays there convulsing on the ground. I won't finish them off; I'll leave their fresh, bloody meat for the hungry coyotes.

I look back through the sights for the SUV and see the SUV and it's stopped. Seems like they're debating where to go. I use a signal mirror to contact the driver, and as I look through the scope, I can see he's spotted me. The driver is dressed in what looks like my enemy's military clothing and is wearing a burka around his face. I signal again and stand up so he can see me. When I look through my scope again, he is looking at me and starts to drive toward me. My blood is really pumping, first from the shooting and second because I now have someone coming here to maybe help me get out of here.

I limp down to the ground floor and open the main gate, a large, metal one that has seen better days; it has a few large holes and a lot of bullet holes but still it will stop anyone or any vehicle from entering. My adrenaline is still pumping and I feel no pain. I stand there with my sniper rifle in hand, hoping this person will be a good guy and not the enemy, because the enemy was chasing him and trying to kill him, he must be good to go.

The SUV pulls up to the gate, and I have my weapon at the ready. The driver's window is already down, and one arm is out of the window, as if to say they come in piece. I hear from his covered face, "Don't shoot, don't shoot, thank you, thank you." It's a woman, and she sounds exhausted.

I tell her to pull in, and I shut the gate behind her. It's a woman! I'm not taking any chances and go over and open the driver door with my weapon pointed at her. I tell her to get out, and I pull her to the ground face down. I tell her, "Arms out and don't move." I look inside the vehicle and see a bloody knife in the front seat, and then I open the back door and see an unconscious woman who is curled up; there's blood all over the seat.

I begin to search the lady on the ground and ask her, "What is your name?" She begins to cry. I say again in a louder, firm voice, "What is your name?" She replies, "Anna."

"Anna, why are you running from those men?" "Those were very bad men, and they tried to kill us for leaving them. Thank you for saving me and my cousin, we were barely able to escape!" Anna was still laying face first on the ground, and I took off the scarf wrapped around her face. As she looks back at me, I see she is strikingly beautiful, with dark eyes and long black hair.

I finish searching her and ask, "Who is the woman in the car with you?" She replies, "That's my cousin, Asha." "How long ago did she get shot?" "Maybe half an hour ago, or less." "Okay, Anna, come help me get her out of the car."

We get Asha out of the car and lay her body on the ground. I take her scarf off and feel for air from her nose; she is still breathing, but I look and see that there is blood coming from her leg and stomach. Anna's eyes begin to tear up, and I tell her, "Look, we need to move her over to a room just inside the warehouse." I grab Asha under her shoulders, and Anna grabs her feet. We lift her and take her to a table and lay her on it. Asha cries out in pain and she is barely alive.

I begin to cut off her bloody clothes. There is a large hole in her thigh with small amount of blood coming out, but it doesn't look like the bullet hit an artery. I tell Anna to take one of the bandages that I laid on the table; I always carry some on me in case of emergency. I tell her to open it up and put direct pressure on the wound. I look over at the stomach area as I cut open her shirt with my knife. Her stomach looks very bad: there is a hole and a few intestines that are sticking out. I look at Anna and say, "I'll do the best I can."

I look for exit wounds and see one that came out just under the backside of the bottom of the rib cage. The leg also has an exit wound, and I say this is a good thing because the bullets aren't inside her.

I take a water bottle, wash the intestines off, and put them back inside her. I clean the blood around the wound and put a pressure dressing on, and then I do the same for the bullet wound and the exit wounds on her leg and backside. I have some morphine and IV bags and tell Anna to wait there. I go to a locker, grab the things I need, and give her a shot and start her IV. Then I begin to tightly wrap her stomach up. After I'm finished, I say to Anna, "Your cousin is now stable, but we'll need to find medical help fast, or she might not make it." I look into Anna's eyes and try to sound convincing. "You are safe here, and everything will be okay. Wait here; I want to go and see if there are more men following. I'll only be a minute." I grab the sniper rifle. As I start walking for the gate, I look back and can see Anna with her head close to Asha's, whispering words into her ear.

I look out at the two armor vehicles, and in the distance I can see the men I shot still on the ground but not moving. Maybe they won't be alive when the coyotes come. Without seeing anyone else, I go back down to where Anna is and say, "There is no one following."

It's starting to get dark, and I make Anna and Asha a couple beds. We all head upstairs to my room. As night falls and it's time to try to get some sleep, I lay down the booby traps and make one last perimeter check before checking on the two women. I keep a small light on in the room, so I can check on them periodically.

I lie in bed hoping everything will be okay tonight. I'm very exhausted, one of my wounds has opened up, and now I have two women to worry about. I hope maybe we can leave soon, now that there's a vehicle. I look over at Anna, who's standing over and taking care of Asha. Anna reminds me of someone I have seen before, but it's hard to tell from where.

As soon as I am about to fall asleep, I feel that cold breeze again over my bed, and it overtakes my body. I try to say something, but nothing comes out! I look out of the corner of my eye and can see Anna. She is standing, and I can see her facing me and screaming something, but I can't hear anything. Then I lose consciousness.

I wake up to Anna shaking me. She's asking me, "Are you okay? Do you know what that was?"

I say, "It was here before. I didn't know if it was real or if I was dreaming, I've always been alone. There is a cold feeling that comes over me, and then I feel paralyzed, and then I see it in my dreams. **I call it Delta.** It's the face that has come to my dreams, the face of the enemy body from downstairs that I killed a week or so ago. I tried to burn the body, but it won't catch fire.

"The strangest thing is I feel that it helped save me from the burning vehicle I was in when we were attacked, when I tried to leave this place. Somehow I made it out alive and when I came to, I was back here in the warehouse. Did you see it? What did it look like?"

Anna replies in a calm voice, "It won't be back, but we will have to leave here very soon."

CHAPTER 3

THE ESCAPE

I awake and see light coming from outside. I look over at the two women: to my surprise Anna is still awake, watching over me and Asha. I sit up and ask Anna, "How are you?"

Anna walks over to me and replies, "I'm okay. How are you? Are you ready to get out of here?" "Yes, I am!" I said "First let me go around the perimeter and make sure everything looks okay." I grab my sniper rifle and look over at Asha, who is lying in her bed. "Will Asha be okay to travel?" Anna says, "Yes, she'll be okay."

I grab my weapon and leave out the door, disarming the booby traps as I go, and then I walk around the perimeter. I make it to the lookout area and look into the distance with my scope from my rifle, spotting some coyotes; I know those soldiers that I left alive had a gruesome death last night.

I leave the lookout area and walk downstairs, going by the SUV Anna was driving. I notice a big puddle of anti-freeze under the vehicle. I open the hood and see there is a large bullet hole in the radiator, where fluid has leaked out, but the good thing is, it still should be able to drive to the other vehicles before it overheats, and then I can drive one of them out of here.

I make my way back inside and pass by Delta and the burned bodies. He lies there and has a different grin on his face. Goosebumps rise on my arms. It is a very eerie feeling being around this Delta, I do not ever want to have to come back here again.

I walk closer to Delta and look at his inhuman face. I say to him, "I know there is a spirit in you, an evil one, and I know you can hear me. I'm going to leave this place and help these two woman that have somehow come to me. These woman are in my hands now, and we are getting out of this unholy place "alive! And I will die trying to save them."

I turn to walk away and feel the wind pick up; there is a cold breeze, but I pay no attention and go up the stairs to Anna and Asha, who are there waiting for me. I tell Anna, "There are some MREs over there. Take what you like." I walk over to Asha, who is lying on the bed with her eyes open, and I say to Anna, "Is she ready?" I look over at her wounds, and they are wrapped tight and well enough to travel and get her out of here.

Anna says, "Yes, she is ready! Now it's your turn, please sit down; I want to look at you." I sit on a chair next to Asha's bed, and Anna goes over my bandages. She takes two of the bandages off and begins to clean my wounds, and then she wraps them back up. I say, "Thank you, you are a pro." She laughs and replies, "We have to keep you healthy, and yes, you can say that I am somewhat of a pro."

I reply "Let me gather a few things. Also, your vehicle is damaged, but the good thing is it will make it to the other vehicles that were following you. Hopefully their Humvees will be fine enough to drive, and we can get the hell out of here." Anna seems to get a very angry look on her face as she stares at me, but she refrains from saying anything. I say, "Don't worry, everything will be fine. I want to leave here soon, so eat something and get your things in order, and we'll leave in fifteen minutes."

I gather more ammo, another weapon that's lying around, and a backpack of food and many water bottles. I ask Anna, "Are you ready to go?" "Yes, we can't wait to get out of here." I grab Asha and put her over my shoulder very carefully, trying not to rip her stomach back open, and we head down the stairs. We get to the vehicle, and I can tell Asha is in a lot of pain; she looks very pale. I lay her down in the back seat of the vehicle and say, "Asha, everything will be okay, just hang in there for a little while longer."

Anna tends to Asha for a minute as I start the vehicle and then open the gate. I say to the woman, "We don't have much time; it's very hot outside, and the vehicle will overheat soon."

Anna stays in the back seat with Asha, and I look around outside. Everything is clear, and I waste no time heading toward the other vehicles. I pray that Delta will not follow and allow me and the woman to leave peacefully.

After five minutes of driving slow, and with ten minutes more to reach the other vehicles, the car starts to overheat and smoke comes out of the radiator. I hope we can make it. The vehicle continues to smoke, and the temperature gauge is over the red line. It's just a matter of time, and then the vehicle's engine freezes up.

I say, "We're not far from one of the vehicles. Stay here." I give Anna one of my pistols. "Do you know how to use this?"

"Yes, I've used them before." I think to myself, "I bet you have. You are not an average women." Then I say to her, "If something happens to me, get to one of these vehicles and head west. We have one of our bases about fifty miles from here, and you will be safe there."

I take my sniper rifle and look toward the closer Humvee. I don't see anything moving. I can see the head of the driver, who has a large bullet hole that took part of his face off, but I can't see the other shooters. I look out to the farther Humvee and don't see any movement. I take my sniper rifle, sling it around my back, and grab my AK before walking cautiously toward the Humvee.

As I slowly make my way to the vehicle, I see one of the shooters; he has a huge hole in his stomach and is missing part of his arm and legs. The coyotes and buzzards got to him. A few feet away I see the other soldier, who has part of his head missing, and his clothes are torn as if the coyotes had also feasted on him.

I make it to the vehicle and go around the passenger door, then around to the driver's door, opening it and pulling the dead driver out. I reach in and try to start the vehicle, but it won't turn over. I look at the fuel gauge, and there is no fuel left. When I had shot the driver and the vehicle stopped, the engine never shut off and used up all the fuel. I get out and go to the back of the Humvee to see if there are any fuel cans, but there isn't. "It figures. This couldn't be easy!"

I take my sniper rifle and look through the scope to the farther vehicle; there are fuel jugs in the back. I started to get a little excited; maybe we'll get out of here yet. I look back at Anna, who is watching me. I raise my arm across my neck as if to signal nothing is here, and then I motion with my arm to the other vehicle.

It's a five-minute walk to the other vehicle. As I'm walking to it, I notice a half-eaten arm; it must have been the arm I shot off, and the coyotes got to it. I get close to the Humvee and cautiously approach it. I remember there was a driver that I shot in the chest, and one I shot in the head, and one I shot his arm off. I look around with the scope and can see the shooter with his head blown off, and I can see the dead driver slouched over . . . but I still can't see the other shooter whose arm I shot.

I make it to the vehicle and take a quick look inside before looking around for the other shooter. He must be here somewhere. I go around the vehicle, giving it a wide berth, and still see no one, but I do notice a dried-up blood trail leading to the Humvee. I wonder if the soldier didn't die last night; maybe he was alive and took shelter inside?

Now my blood pleasure has risen. What to do? What is the safest way to go about this? I have a grenade; maybe I can throw it inside of the vehicle. But as I think for a moment, I hear a noise. I draw my weapon, ready to shoot. I stop and hold my breath, and I hear it again—it's coming from under the vehicle. I move fast, taking cover behind a large rock a few feet away and pointing my weapon under the vehicle.

I take aim and can see someone is under there. My heart is racing—SHIT! I could have been killed. The soldier is looking at me, and I can hear him saying, "Help me." I can't see if he has any weapons, and I know he has only one arm and is in bad shape. I go over to the vehicle with my weapon pointed at him; reaching under and pulling him out. He is barely alive. I say, "What is your name?"

"Kalvin." "Kalvin! Why were you chasing those women?" He says in his dry, scratchy voice, "Are they alive?" I said yes, and he smiles and starts to laugh a little. I don't know what to think—a dying man laughing? "Those are very bad woman; watch out for them, especially Anna. They betrayed us, and they are your enemy and ours."

He starts to cough, and blood pours from his mouth. He says, "You will see. You must kill them both!" He is barely able to speak out, but he manages to say, "Anna, you must kill her!" He takes his last breath and is dead.

A chill comes over me, and I wonder, "What the hell did he mean? Did Anna and Asha have to get away from these bad men . . . or is there something else going on?"

Worried that the vehicle is booby-trapped on the inside, I take the two fuel containers off the back and walk to the other Humvee. I pour the fuel in and then start the vehicle. And for the first time in a while, I smile. I hope it's enough to get to the base or close enough to it, because both Asha and I are in need of serious medical attention.

I drive to the SUV where Anna and Asha are waiting. As I pull up, I only see Asha lying in the back seat, sweating profusely. There's no sign of Anna. Now my slight happiness has gone to angry and worried. I ask Asha, "Where is Anna?" She replies, "I don't know. She said to me, 'Everything will be okay,' and she left!" I said angrily, "Did she say anything else?" Asha has tears in her eyes and says, "No, nothing."

I look around and don't see Anna anywhere. I take my sniper rifle and look through the scope and still nothing. Then I look toward the warehouse and notice that the front gate is shut. I say to myself, "This can't be. Has Anna gone back for something? Why couldn't she just fucking wait for me? We have to get out of here." It's now around 11:00 a.m., and it's getting very hot, maybe 130 degrees. We have to get moving, otherwise Asha will surly dehydrate, get heat stroke, and die.

I think again for a moment and wonder whether I should leave Anna behind, but another side of me says she came to me for a reason. I can't leave her behind. I make a decision that I may regret: I will go find Anna, and then we all will all leave here together.

We drive over to the warehouse and find a place in the shade and parked. I pull out an IV bag and hook Asha up to it. I look at Asha and grab her hand. Then I pull out a pistol and give it to her. "If you need this, it's here. I will be back soon, so don't worry."

I try the gate but it's locked. "How could the gate be locked? Something's not right." But I knew another way in, a spot where I found a coyote sneaking in one night. I go to that spot, quietly move the piece of metal covering the hole, and go in. I have a very airy feeling once I enter, it is very quiet. I listen for any noise coming from Anna, I but just hear the sound of the dusty wind blowing and the noise of a couple pieces of loose metal banging around. I make my way inside, and still no sign of Anna. "Shit, where could she be?" Then I think, "Maybe she is with that Delta."

I make my way around the upstairs of the warehouse to get a view of where the Delta was laying. When I get to where I can see, I notice Delta but no sign of Anna. Now I was wonder, "Was she even here? Did I come back here for nothing? Or did she get bit by a snake? Somewhere she is lying helpless, and I didn't see her, and the wind might have blown the gate shut." Now I was getting mad.

As I get up to leave, I hear something, so I stop and wait. I see a shadow, something is down there. I wait another few minutes, but I can't see it and don't hear anything. Is my mind playing tricks on me? I have to move closer and be sure before I leave here, but the only closer view is downstairs and close to Delta's room.

I'm going to take the chance. I quietly make my way down there, and it takes almost five minutes. I find a spot about thirty feet away. I can now see Delta, but I don't see anything else. I wait a few more minutes and still nothing. I wonder about Asha, she has to get to safety, and Anna may be dead or dying out there in the desert. "Two more minutes, and if there is nothing, then I'm leaving," I say to myself. I look at my watch and wait. It's so hot, and I have nonstop sweat dripping down my face.

"Must have been nothing," I angrily mumble, and I get up to leave. Then I hear a voice, perhaps a woman's voice, echoing through the empty walls of this place. But where can it be coming from? Anna must be here. I make my way closer, and now I'm only twenty feet from Delta, but now I can see everything.

There is Anna . . . and she's digging a hole?

CHAPTER 4

THE ENEMY'S LAIR

I'm very upset. I look around the area, and there is no one else, only Anna. I walk to her and pay no attention to where Delta lies. I stand there for a second, and Anna still doesn't see me. I say her name loudly.

She smiles, says, "I knew you'd come back," and continues digging. I have goose bumps that chill my body, and I say, "Anna, are you okay? Why are you here? We have to get out of here!" "I must give him a proper burial." She replies in a trance of a voice

I say, "For who? What are you talking about, Anna? Didn't you hear me? We have to go, now!" She looks at Delta and then to me, and she smiles again. "It's not for him—it's for you!" "For me? Have you gone mad? Let's go." Anna says, "The one you call Delta is going to be coming with me and Asha, and *you* will be the one staying here."

I yell, "You don't know what you're talking about! He has some kind of control over you." Then I look at Delta and raise my weapon and fire shots into his head and body. After I'm finished, I look back toward Anna. As I turn my head, I see a shadow coming for my face and then everything goes black.

I wake and lie there motionless, unable to move, as I did the times before when Delta came into my dreams. I am in the grave Anna dug, and my hands and feet are tied. The grave's not very deep but is deep enough to cover me.

I can barely see out of the hole, and I see Anna over by Delta. She is saying something to him. I say, "This can't be happening; maybe it's only a bad dream! Maybe I'm still outside, and I blacked out from the heat and am dreaming all this." But as blood trickles down my face, I know I'm not dreaming. I yell to Anna, "Anna, come here." She looks back at me and comes quickly toward me, looking very upset. "What is going on? Why you are doing this? Fight whatever urges you to stay here, and let's get out of here. I have Asha in the vehicle outside, and we are all set to leave this place."

Anna comes closer to me and raises the shovel as if she is going to strike me again. I say, "Anna, wait! Why are you doing this? I saved you from those bad men". Anna starts to laugh and says, "Those men, those pieces of shit men! They were trying to stop me from coming here. You are a fool!" I remember the man's face as he said, "They are bad, especially Anna." I said, "Why then?"

"He is my general. He came to me in my dream and said he was in trouble, and I should come get him. He said you were the one who killed him; I felt it when I first met you. Now that I have a running vehicle and can leave safely and now with Delta, I will leave you here to die." She laughs. "You will lie here helpless in your grave, and then the coyotes will come for you when they smell your dying body."

Anna then strikes down at my head with the shovel, and I fall into the darkness of night.

I awake and am lying here with a horrible headache, and I can feel fresh and dried blood all over my face. I start to get my bearings back, and I remember I have a small knife inside the back part of my belt. I feel for it and am thankful it's still there as I use it to cut these ropes off. I can hear coyotes in the distance; in a short time they will be coming, and I hope there are some weapons around!

I am freed from the ropes and wiggle through the dirt to get out of my grave, there is very little light from the moon. I remember in one of the rooms close by, there are a few broken up weapons from the fallen soldiers. I stumble around and am able to find the room and grab an AK that has a broken stock but it will do the trick then I feel for bullets; the weight of the magazine seems to have enough to do what I need to. I can hear the coyotes getting closer. I know there is a table in the room, and I feel for it, grabbing it and pulling it with me to the corner of the room. I put the table in front of me and use it as a shield.

Five minutes or so go by, and in the pitch black room I wait patiently. The coyotes are coming, and I can hear them walking. They're breathing hard and have my scent from the fresh blood. They are thinking it's an easy meal, but not this time. I hear them get close, there in the room. There must be three or four, and I fire around the room and hear a few yelps as some run away. I wait for a few minutes and don't hear anything moving, so I make my way quickly out of the warehouse.

I'm on a mission: whatever it takes, I will find Anna and kill her and that fucking Delta, and nothing is going to get in my way! I remember the Humvee and make my way to it. It's dark out, but the moonlight is enough, so I can see my way. It takes about thirty minutes of steady walking, but I make it.

At the vehicle I say a quick prayer as I open the driver door and feel for any type of tension, but there is none; it's not booby trapped, and I'm very relieved. I hope the vehicle will start, otherwise it will be a long walk, which I'm ready to make if need be. I reach in and try to start the Humvee, and thank God it started. When I shot the driver, his momentum must have hit the kill button and killed the engine.

I take the dead soldier from the driver seat and pull him out and look around for the man I had shot in the head. I take his uniform and put it on, and then I use my tattered clothes to wipe any blood and guts that are still on the seat.

I know there is a small town nearby. Anna had only so much fuel and couldn't get far, so they must have headed there. The only problem is it's in enemy's territory! At this point I don't care, I will kill whoever is in my way. I start to drive toward the town, and twenty-five minutes later I enter it. I find a street kid and ask if he has seen a vehicle like the one that I'm driving, and he says "Yes, that belongs to the soldiers. They're there, in that building."

I see the other Humvee and know this is the place that Anna went. I hide my vehicle and go into the building, using a side door. There is a small celebration going on inside as I look around. I can see Anna as she is drinking with some soldiers at a table. There are some stairs going up, and I decide I'll look around for a minute. I make my way upstairs, and at the far end of a long hallway there is one door that is guarded by a soldier.

There is a room to my right, and I go into it. It's a lab of some sort, and there are five beds with bodies in them hooked up to IVs of blood. "What is this place?" I whisper to myself. Then I exit and walk toward the guard, saying to him as I approach, "It's my turn for watch." But the guard sees the marks on my face and some blood on my uniform, so I hurry to take my knife out, grab him, and cut his throat, bringing him into the room with me.

The room is dark, the only light coming from some candles. I can see Asha on a bed looking in bad shape, and then I see Delta. He is on another bed and has an IV of blood going into him. I question myself, "He's dead! These people must all be crazy!"

I remember I gave Asha a pistol, and I walk over and put my hand over her mouth to suffocate her. I'm not taking any chances. I feel her last breath, and then I search her. Under her pillow is my pistol. I put it back in the back of my belt and walk over to Delta, who's lying there with his eyes closed. I have a feeling that he knows I'm here.

I can hear someone coming! I grab my AK and have it ready to fire, and I look around to take cover. But there is no place to go, so I hurry and hide behind the door. The door flies open, and two guards come in followed by Anna. Anna goes and gives attention to Delta as the guards stand there and watch.

I'm now standing behind the two guards. I surprise them when I say, "Don't fucking move." The guards and Anna look back at me and are surprised to see me with an AK facing them. I close the door and tell the guards, "Put down your weapons," and they do so.

Anna looks at me and says in an angered voice, "This can't be, I knew I should have killed you." "Yes, you should have!" I take the butt of my AK and hit each guard in the back of the head, knocking them out. As they lie motionless on the floor, I take out my knife as I look at Anna, and I cut their throats. Anna walks quickly to Asha and sees that she is dead. Then she reaches under the pillow and feels around.

I say loudly, "Don't bother, I already have it. Anna, why are you giving Delta blood?" She says, "There is a lot you don't know about, and you have seen too much already." "Then you're going to have to tell me everything!"

CHAPTER 5

A NEW BEGINNING

Anna laughs and says, "You want to know everything? Okay then, since you've made it this far in the adventure, I will tell you.

"Delta, as you call him, is our military leader, our general. How you killed, or stopped him, I should say, you were very lucky, as well as killing off his team. I do give you a lot of credit for that! We called that team the Unstoppables! Nobody has been any challenge to them, and they are the ones we were counting on to win this war. We had a scientist who taught me all of his secrets, and I was his special assistant." Anna gave a little laugh. "This scientist did many experiments during the Vietnam War, funded by governments as he tried to make an enhanced fighting soldier. But when the experiments went wrong and the soldiers lost all their mental realities and changed their physical appearances, the project was instantly dropped. When he heard that the experiments and all involved were being exterminated, this scientist immediately went into hiding on a private island, where he continued his experiments.

"Over the years he was able to perfect his experiments, turning those who were once ordinary into his ultimate killing machines. He was funded by some of the same governments who at that time wanted him exterminated, and that is where he got his supply of soldiers to experiment on. He retained some of his biggest clients and funding.

"He would sell off his creatures as buyers would watch the tournaments he held on his island. The buyers would watch while in his luxury mansion, as his creatures would hunt and kill the players of the card tournaments.

But he got careless. Some of the agencies got word of him still being alive and selling his creatures, and eventually they found out he was holding these tournaments. They wanted an end to it all. It all came to an end when a player named Bill, who was with the CIA, infiltrated a card tournament as one of those players. I don't know how he did it, usually no one makes it off the island alive. His island was then taken over, and everything he worked on was lost. He managed to escape by letting his creatures out, buying him enough time to make a safe getaway and to destroy all of his rooms filled with his experiments and secrets.

That island is where I learned about these creatures and his secrets. I would act as a sexy hostess and welcome the players when they would gather at the boat dock. Then I would take the players to the island, and little did the players know what they were getting themselves into. I sure did! It was very interesting to observe them from before they first entered the mansion, till they were set out for the night's survival activities. Their lives and personalities changed in a matter of minutes.

I would get a special tour with the scientist himself and view his new creatures for upcoming tournaments, and I would pick my favorite creature to win. "Winning" was which creature best hunted down the groups and killed the most players. It was fun! And at the end of the tournament, that creature would go up for bidding and would draw millions. It was very profitable, as betters and buyers would come from all over the world and watch in secrecy in the mansion, via cameras. They would also bet on the players—how long they could survive, who would win, those sorts of things. It was very educational, to say the least.

"When he was run off his paradise island, I took him in. He had nowhere to go, and we were able to provide him his safety. In agreement he would teach me, and I would learn and carry out all of his secrets. We worked day and night for months, and many experiments were done on our soldiers, as well as your soldiers that we captured. Our biggest achievement was that the chemicals in the past would collect in the eyes and stain them, causing the eyes to give a glowing appearance. I was able to change all that!

"One day, we found the perfect mixture and the perfect candidate. Delta, as you like to call him, took to the substances immediately, and his body thrived on the chemicals. As he took more and more, he became unstoppable. He has the physical look of any man but the strength and powers of no man alive. He also possesses mind capabilities as well, and that's the secret of how he came to you in your dreams.

"This was the first successful group we had put together, and Delta was the best of the group. He was the new leader, the general! We have rooms full of men right now taking the chemical, becoming our new ultimate fighting soldiers. Once these soldiers receive their first blood transfusion, they immediately have an unstoppable drive, and after months of taking this chemical, killing them is almost impossible! The soldier's blood runs thick with this special blood, and it will regenerate in time and bring them back to life. Because Delta took the blood for so long, that is why he will not burn, he has evolved! That is also why he can still be brought back.

"You were keeping our little secrete, and we had to get it back. The reason the soldiers tried to stop us is because they call us the unholies, and we take them at random and give them these special chemicals. We want everyone to have this power.

Asha and I would have been stopped, they almost killed us. But if it wasn't for you saving us from those traitors, this would have all come to an end, and I want to thank you for that. "Now, since you know so much, maybe you will like to receive power similar to Delta's?" "No! I don't want any part of your unholy madness! What happened with the professor?"

Anna replies with a smirk on her face, "**The professor?** You mean The Man?" She laughs again. "He wanted only a special group of creatures and not a whole army. He only wanted to sell his special creatures to the highest bidders. But he couldn't have advanced his special chemicals without me! He got jealous and was very deceitful when I said I wanted to build the strongest army in the world, using these special soldiers to take over whatever I wanted. I could not take any chances. It is my mission and destiny to take. Once the chemicals started to work on the soldiers, and I now had Delta and knew the special compounds . . . I took off his head, Even though the professor was my father!"

"Your father?"

"Yes, that's right! I could not let him or his secrets fall into anyone else's hands, like it almost did when he was on his island. I did, however, keep a few of his special creatures; after many experiments they lost their human form, and there was no changing them back. But they kept such incredible strengths and powers that I did not want to kill them. I have them kept in a special place, to be used for a special occasion."

Saying loudly to Anna, "Not this time, Anna. All this madness will end here and now! I now hold the power to kill you and Delta. Now I know where I have seen you!" Anna looks back with a puzzled look on her face. "You don't know me, you don't know anything about me!"

I reply, "Yes, I do! You where the one at the boat dock eight years ago, dressed in your little sexy white outfit. You and your cousin Asha were the two hostesses. You look a little different now, maybe grown up, maybe more matured and evil. You don't recognize me because of my beard and military clothes. I was there at the boat dock. I also was also on that island, even in that mansion, and I also met your father, The Man. I also meet his creatures firsthand."

"Were you someone from one of the government agencies, buying creatures from my father?" "You can say I was from one of the government agencies."

Anna has a disturbed look on her face and an odd pitch in her voice. "I don't believe you. Then which agency?" "I was with the CIA, and I was also the one who took down your father's empire. My name is Bill! I'm glad The Man is finished, and when I kill you, this family empire of yours will be destroyed, and all this madness will be over."

Anna says, "I'm sorry Bill, is that your real name?" "I haven't gone by that name in so long. These days I call myself Michael." Anna starts walking around the room and says in a confident voice, "How interesting, Bill, I mean Michael. I can't believe destiny brought you here again to me. And you are already practically family, knowing all the secrets of the family's empire. But you cannot finish me or our plans!" "Our plans'?"

Anna stops walking as everything seems to become clear to her and she looks up with a smile on her face. "I now know I have plans for you, Michael. Big plans!" She points to the corners of the ceiling. "Did you see those cameras? I didn't think so!" Outside in the hall are twenty men." As if on cue, the door flies open, and a split second soldiers are all in the room, running in front of Delta and Anna as shields. The others surround me with their weapons pointed.

One comes from behind, and a hard hit to the back of my head, then there is blackness. I awake in a bed, with an IV going into me. Anna is standing over me, and I am strapped down, my arms to my side.

She bends down and then gives me a kiss on my lips. "You will be my special project. When I'm finished with you, you might even be my new general!" Looking over I see the blood bag and tubes coming down into my veins. I pass out again, and then wake up delusional. There are now four empty blood bags and a fresh one, and I pass out again.

Awakening in a dark room; I'm standing and am now free to move. There is some light from under a door, and it stinks of rotting flesh in here. I hear a noise coming from behind me, and then I am hit hard from behind and fall face first to the floor. Whatever that is, it's hiding in the darkness.

I hear it coming again. This time I feel its movements, and I block its strike and move in and flip him over me with surprising ease. I wait for him to strike again and sense him as he is going around the room, using the darkness as cover. I can hear what he is thinking, his heart beating. He tenses as he is going to strike, and he comes from behind. I duck, and he falls over me. Quickly grabbing his head and pulling him down in front of me, I grab for his throat with no hesitation and pull it out. He is dead, and I stay still, trying to feel if someone else is in here. There is no one else. Then there is a bad smell, and I awake dressed in a nice uniform, sitting behind a desk.

It's dark in front of me, and then the lights go on. There are three people sitting silent in front of me, dressed in nice black suits. It's a large room, and there's nothing but me, the three men, and the chairs all sitting around my desk. There is a deep harsh sounding voice coming from a speaker. "Carefully look at these men and find out who is a traitor?" "I do not understand," I say back.

The loud voice replies, "One of these men tried to give secrets to the enemy. I want you to figure which one and kill him." Staring for a silent moment and looking deep into the eyes of each man, I can feel they are all scared but well composed. I can hear and feel their heartbeats and I see their pupils dilating as they're breathing harder. I can hear their thoughts as I look deeper at each one.

The first one has nothing to hide; he is calm but scared. The second is scared, but it's not him. I look at the third one and feel that he is hot; his blood is pumping harder, but he looks calm. I feel for his thoughts and can sense that he is afraid. I can hear as he is talking with people about very important information to give them, and then it ends—I have made my decision!

I get up and walk behind the three men, going back and forth a few times. I notice there is a baseball bat in the corner, and I grab it. "Don't move," I say in calm manner and I take one step back and wait a few seconds. I feel a heightened tension in the room, it's so overwhelming! I can picture myself sitting there as one of these men.

Their feelings, their adrenaline, their fear, I can feel it all! Then I raise my bat and without hesitation hit the third man hard in the back of the head, causing his brains and skull to go all over.

The voice comes over the speaker and says, "Very well done!" The two others are asked to get up and leave. I take my bat and walking behind the desk I sit down. The door opens and the two men leave, and then a woman comes in and hangs a picture on the wall. She is very beautiful and sits down, not caring that there is a dead body there. She asks me, "Do you remember me?" Looking deep into my eyes with an eagerness of what I am going to say. I sit and look at her for a minute, and nothing comes to mind, only a sensation, neither happy nor hatred. "No I reply."

She says, "My name is Anna, and you have turned into a very special soldier!" Then she asks, "Do you know your name?" I look around and then focus on the picture of me on the wall, with a military style uniform on. At the bottom it says, "General Michael Striker."

I reply, "My name is General Michael Striker." She replies, "That's correct. Why are you here?"

I say back with a confident tone, "to do as you say and to kill anyone who stands in our way!" She smiles and says, "That's correct!"

To Be Continued!